MW01092598

DEATH IN THE BAY

A Cedar Bay Cozy Mystery - Book 17

BY

DIANNE HARMAN

CONTENTS

ACKNOWLEDGMENTS

Thank you, Tom, for everything you do to make me look good. I hope you know how much I appreciate it.

Win FREE Paperbacks every week!

Go to www.dianneharman.com/freepaperback.html and get your FREE copies of Dianne's books and favorite recipes immediately by signing up for her newsletter.

Once you've signed up for her newsletter you're eligible to win three paperbacks. One lucky winner is picked every week. Hurry before the offer ends!

PROLOGUE

"Kelly, I'm going to be late tonight. Greg wants to talk to me. We're going to have a drink at The Waterfront. I should be home by seven. Can you hold dinner until then?" Mike asked.

"Sure. What's the topic?" Kelly asked, curiously.

"I have no idea. He said something has been bothering him, and he needs to get it off his chest. Fortunately, everything is calm here at the sheriff's station right now, so I won't have a problem getting out of here a little early."

"Okay. Tell him hi for me, and I'll see you later."

*****

"Hi, Greg, Mike. Greg, same table as usual?" Sam, the affable owner of The Waterfront Restaurant, asked.

"That would be great, however I won't be staying for dinner, so I don't want you to waste a table on us. We'll just sit at one of the bar tables."

"Take your pick, but I don't know how my servers and the chef will survive. I mean, you're our number one regular customer, you and Susie."

"I know. We're kind of a legend in our own time," Greg said with a chuckle. "Not only is your food and service excellent, I love to drive over here in my boat and tie up at your dock. Ever so much easier than fighting the traffic on the highway," he said with a wink.

"Right. Like we've got a lot of traffic in sleepy little Cedar Bay. Well, enjoy your drinks. Mitzi will be over in a minute to get your order."

Mike and Greg sat down at the table and before they could say a word, they heard Mitzi say, "Greg, Mike, glad you were seated at one of my tables. By the way, Mike, my nephew is thinking about a career in law enforcement. Okay if he calls and makes an appointment to talk to you? I figured as the sheriff, you could tell him what to expect better than anyone else could."

"Of course, Mitzi. Have him give my secretary a call to make an appointment. Glad he's interested in it."

"All right, gentlemen. Now that we've got the important stuff out of the way, what can I get you?"

"I'd like a beer," Mike said.

"Got a preference?" Mitzi asked.

"No, whatever you have on tap will be fine."

"You got it." She turned to Greg and said, "Greg what'll it be for you? The usual? Scotch on the rocks?"

"That's it. Thanks."

"Okay Greg, what's on your mind?" Mike asked.

Greg was quiet while Mitzi placed their drinks in front of them and then he began to speak. "Mike, this is really uncomfortable for me. You've known me ever since we were in college and one of the reasons I moved up here after I retired was to live near you."

"Nice words, my friend, but we both know the real attraction was Cedar Bay itself. It's one of the few places along the West Coast where you can take your boat out and enjoy it without being overrun by a crowd. Plus the fact that an amazing house right on the waterfront was up for sale, and you bought it for a song. But I do appreciate your kind words," Mike said with a grin.

"All right, you know me too well." He ran his fingers through his hair in a sign of frustration. "Mike, I don't know how to say this other than straight out. I've been seeing Doc Burkham because I haven't felt very good for the last couple of months." He took a deep breath. "I have cancer, and unfortunately, not the good kind."

"I didn't know there was a good kind of cancer," Mike said, trying to keep the solemnity of Greg's words from sinking in.

"Yeah, I suppose the words good kind and cancer shouldn't be said in the same breath. Anyway, it's pancreatic cancer."

"Oh, man, I am so sorry."

"Yeah, I'm not exactly jumping up and down with joy over the diagnosis and the prognosis sucks. Doc told me the one-year survival rate is 25% and the five-year survival rate is only 6%. Let's put it this way. You know I love Vegas, but those are some of the lousiest odds I've ever run across. I sure wouldn't place any bets on me surviving."

Mike was quiet for several long moments and then said, "Have you told Susie yet?"

"No." He paused while he took a long drink. "Actually, I'd been thinking of divorcing her." He looked at Mike who had a stunned look on his face and said, "Don't look so shocked. You know that marrying her was one of the biggest mistakes I've ever made. Quite frankly, our marriage has been dead for quite a while, but with this diagnosis, and based on the future, it doesn't make any sense to do it now."

"Yeah, you probably don't need any added stress right now."

"No, that's for sure, and I sure as heck don't need to give her half my assets, which she'd get in divorce court. Mike, I've appointed you as trustee of my trust. The way it stands now Susie gets 1/3 of my estate and each of my kids, Jessica, and Scott, get 1/3."

"Sounds pretty straight up. I can handle that," Mike said.

"Yeah, on paper it sounds good, but here's the deal. I have an appointment in a few days with Lem Bates, you know, the local attorney here in town. He's helped me with a couple of other things, and I'm going to have him redo my trust. The one I presently have was drawn up by my attorney in San Francisco just after Susie and I got married."

"And I assume Susie is not going to be the recipient of 1/3 of your new trust. Would I be right?"

"Yeah. Not only is she not going to get 1/3 of it, neither is Scott, but first about Susie. I'm about 100% sure she has a boyfriend, and I rather doubt he's the first."

"Oh, Greg, that's lousy. You sure don't need that right now. What makes you think that?"

"Well, she started spending a lot of time at the fitness center we belong to. Originally, we'd go together, but in the last few months, she always had an excuse about why she couldn't go with me, and lately I haven't been going that often because I just didn't feel up to it.

"One day she accidentally left her phone at home, which is something she never does. I think it's kind of like an earring to her, you know, permanently attached to her ear."

"Yeah, I see a lot of people like that," Mike said.

"Well, I happened to see it when I walked by and was curious why she was spending so much time on it. I looked at her recent calls and texts. They were all from someone named Johnny. I put two and two together and figured it must be the trainer stud at the fitness center. I'd guess he's about five or so years younger than she is."

"Greg, I know these things happen in that industry, but a guy working at the fitness center probably has his pick of women. Why choose someone older than him?"

"Money. Pure and simple. Money, or more specifically, my money. I mean Susie is dripping jewelry that I foolishly bought her when we first got together. She's had a lot of work done and looks good for her age, and she drives a brand new Lexus.

"I imagine he thinks there's a lot more where that came from and would probably like to get his hands on it. In case you haven't noticed," he said sarcastically, "being an instructor at a fitness center is not the type of job you can retire on after a few years."

"I'll bet that was a shock. I'm so sorry for you."

"Yeah, well don't be. Be sorry I'm going to die, but don't be sorry about my lousy marriage." He took another long sip of his drink and then looked straight at Mike.

"Quite frankly, I haven't exactly been a choir boy in our marriage. I got tired of living the charade of the marriage I was in and started playing around on the internet, to be specific, on Facebook. The long and short of it is that I found a wonderful woman on one of those dating sites who lives in a nearby town.

"I was looking for something to take my mind off of the debacle of my marriage – which, by the way, I knew was a mistake within a year of marrying Susie. What I wasn't looking for was finding the love of my life, and then finding her too late. When I got Doc's prognosis, I stopped calling her.

"I'm sure I've hurt her, but I knew the truth about my medical condition would hurt Rae Ann more. The reason I'm telling you this is that after I die, I want you to get in touch with her and tell her how much I loved her. I know it will be hard for you, but it might make it easier for her. Will you do that for me?"

"Of course, Greg, whatever you want me to do. I'll need her contact information."

"I'll send it to you. Just tell her what I told you and that I'm sorry."

"You can count on it. Now tell me why you've decided to reduce the amount you were going to give to Scott."

"That kid, well I guess when you're forty-five you're no longer a kid, and his wife spend money like there's no tomorrow. I've already loaned him $100,000, and to the best of my knowledge it went on her back in the form of designer clothes and a leased Mercedes for him. Oh, and did I mention the three-carat solitaire diamond ring she's now wearing?"

"From what you're saying, I'm gathering Jessica is getting the bulk of your estate, which is worth what? Since I'll be settling it, I probably should get an approximate value of your estate."

"When you hear it, don't be shocked. Remember as an only son, I got everything my parents had, and my grandfather had set up a trust for me as well. All told, my estate will be about six million dollars. That includes the house and everything else."

"Wow, Greg, I had no idea it would be that large. How bad are Susie and Scott going to be hurt by a change in the language of your trust?"

"I'm giving each of them 10%, so the remaining 80% goes to Jess. She and her husband have really worked hard for everything they have and never expected a cent from me. As a matter of fact, several times when they were struggling to make a success of his business, I offered to help them, but they refused."

"It always amazes me how kids turn out so differently even though they share the same parents. Maybe I'd understand a little better if I'd had kids, but that part of parenting is a mystery to me," Mike said.

"Obviously, it was to me as well, or I would have done something different. Anyway, it's too late now."

"I guess I should gear myself up to be facing an angry widow and an angry son when the trust is read after your death."

"I didn't feel good about doing that to you, Mike. We go back too far, and quite frankly, it's not your problem. It's kind of one of those 'don't shoot the messenger' things. No, Jess and Scott are both flying into Portland tomorrow. They're renting a car and driving down here.

"I intend to tell them, and Susie, about my prognosis and the trust. I'm sure they're not going to be happy about it, but at least by the time you have to deal with them, they should have accepted it. Plus, a lot of people would think an inheritance of $600,000 was a princely sum.

"Just goes to show you the caliber of the woman I married and the son I raised. Shame to think someone would be upset that they weren't getting two million. Actually, I'd rather spend my energy trying to fight this darned cancer problem than deal with Susie and Scott."

Mike put his hand on Greg's arm. "Greg, why don't you do just that? Spend your time and energy fighting it. If I can deal with hardened criminals, I can probably take on a couple of angry heirs. Let me handle this. Tell them about your illness and then let them take care of you for the time you have left. Don't waste your remaining time dealing with angry family members."

"Thanks, Mike. I appreciate that more than you know, but I couldn't live with myself if I did that. Of course, I won't be living with myself anyway in a few months. No, I'll man up and tell them. I think all three of them will be shocked because there was always the assumption of share and share alike, but that's not fair to Jess."

"You know my feelings for Jess, after all she's my goddaughter," Mike said, "so I can't say I'm sorry that she's getting the lion's share of your estate. What does concern me is that Susie and Scott may be very angry at her, thinking she's getting preferential treatment. Neither one of them seems like people who are particularly introspective, and I rather doubt they'll take the time to think about why you're doing this."

"No, I don't think they will. I'll do whatever I can to allay any anger they may feel towards Jess," Greg said, "but since I still have several months to live according to Doc, by the time I'm gone, they should have accepted it." He finished his drink.

"Mike, I'd love to stay and talk, but I need to get home. The one thing I've found in my fight with cancer, is that I get tired pretty easily. I drove the boat over here, and I don't want to be too tired to drive it back. I've been lucky in that bay. Don't want to spoil it now. Sorry for laying all this on you, but we'll be talking."

"Okay. One last thing, Greg, whatever I can do to help, and I mean anything, no matter how big or small, I want to do it. I'm one phone call away, so just pick it up when you need me. Deal?" he said as he put his hand out for Greg to shake.

"Deal," Greg said, shaking his hand.

As it turned out, that was the last time Mike saw Greg alive, but cancer wasn't the cause of Greg's early demise.

CHAPTER ONE

The following morning Greg looked down at his phone and saw the name "Rae Ann" on the monitor. Even though he had his phone set on silent ring, a habit he'd gotten into when she started calling him, so Susie wouldn't hear his phone ringing, the light from the monitor had caught his attention.

He pressed "Accept" as he walked over to the door of his office and closed it. Susie was taking a yoga class at the fitness center they belonged to, but she might return home at any minute.

"Rae Ann, I've told you never to call me, but here you are once again, like a bad penny showing up. It's over, Rae Ann. Pure and simple, it's over."

"Greg, you may be saying that, but I know you don't mean it. What we had was too good to just let it go. You've told me how bad your marriage is, and that you never want to go through a divorce again, but that doesn't mean we can't still see each other. I promise you I'll never bring up the word 'marriage' again. Honest. I miss you."

Like I don't miss you, Rae Ann, he thought. *You're the best thing that ever happened to me, but it happened too late. You don't know it, but I'm a walking time bomb, and the wick is burning shorter and shorter, according to Doc Burkham. The last thing you need is to get involved with a dying man.*

"Rae Ann, as much as I'd like to see you again, I can't. There are some things going on in my life right now that are pretty traumatic, and I don't want to see you get hurt."

"Greg, what if I were to tell you that I don't care what's going on in your life. All I want is you. Please don't push me away. It's all because of your wife, Susie, isn't it?"

"No, Rae Ann. It isn't that easy. Believe me, I wish it was. Trust me, you're much better off not being with me."

There was silence on the other end of the phone and then Rae Ann said, "Greg, you were the one who contacted me, if you remember. You contacted me on that dating site. You never lied to me. You told me you were married, but there was something intriguing about you, and once I met you, that was it for me. Don't you see that you deserve some happiness? I know I make you happy."

I know Rae Ann, believe me, I know. I hate myself for doing this, but you give me no choice. So long, my beloved, Greg painfully thought.

"Rae Ann, you were nothing more to me than what some would call a one-night stand, actually in our case a few nights' stand, enjoyable, but not long term. I don't love you. I never did. So long. Have a nice life."

He ended the call and put his head in his hands, unbidden tears coursing down his cheeks. He was a good man, but a man who had made mistakes in his past, and like most men, he regretted a few things he'd done. But he'd never regret anything more than what he'd just done to a very fine woman, the woman he wished he'd met many years earlier in life

After a few minutes he heard the front door open, and he quickly wiped his tears away. He plastered a smile on his face, opened the door, and said, "Hi Susie, have a good class?"

*****

Rae Ann stared at the phone in her hand, not believing what Greg had just said. It was very clear from what he'd told her that not only did he not want to see her, he didn't love her, and she was nothing more than a one-night stand type of woman to him.

Rae Ann was in shock. *He was the one who pursued me,* she thought. *He was the one who made all the overtures and kept asking to see me. And then he doesn't call for several days and when I call him, he tells me there are things going on his life.*

What I should have said was "Guess what, Greg? Join the party. I just served my husband divorce papers because of you and now you tell me things are going on your life? Well, what about mine?"

Deep down, she was sure Susie had found out about her and was forcing Greg to give her up. She'd probably threatened him with divorce, and he'd been very firm when he'd said he never wanted to get divorced again because he'd lost so much money in his first two divorces.

He'd told Rae Ann that he'd tried to get Susie to sign a prenup, but she'd refused, so he'd finally given up. Rae Ann had made the decision that she loved him so much she didn't care if he stayed in his marriage. She just wanted him.

She went into the bathroom, hoping splashing some cool water on her wrists would calm her down. Rae Ann looked in the mirror and all she could see was a woman consumed by anger, anger at being cast aside like a piece of old worn-out clothing.

The more she thought about it, the angrier she got. The irony of it didn't escape her. Yesterday she'd had her husband served with divorce papers. Today Greg told her it was over.

Well, she thought, *if I ever doubted that there was such a thing as karma, I no longer do. It just kicked me in the teeth.*

She knew the only reason Greg had said the things he had was because of Susie. The thought of him living the rest of his life with Susie sickened her. What made her even sicker was that Susie had won in the battle for Greg's affections.

Suddenly, as if ideas could be lightning bolts, one came to her out of the blue. It was very simple. If Rae Ann couldn't have Greg, there was no way she'd let Susie have him. She'd rather have Greg dead than have him live the rest of his life with Susie. All that needed to be done was for her to formulate a plan.

And after all, Rae Ann thought, *isn't that what the big companies up and down the West Coast pay me to do? Formulate plans for their companies to be more profitable. Well, this is just a little different from the plans I make for them, but I'm very, very good at making plans, so this should be easy.*

And so she began to plan.

CHAPTER TWO

"This is Kendra, how may I help you?"

"Kendra, it's me, Susie," the tearful voice on the other end of the line said.

"Sorry, Susie, it's been so busy here at work, I just grabbed my phone and never looked at the monitor. I'd ask how you're doing, but I can tell you're not doing all that well. What's up?"

There was such a long silence that Kendra began to wonder if the call had been dropped. "Susie, are you still there?" she asked.

"Yes, I just don't know what to do," Susie said in a teary voice. "How will I ever survive?"

"Susie, take a deep breath. I have no idea what you're talking about. I need you to start at the beginning. And I hate to be a bad sister, but I am at work, and I have a full schedule today. As a matter of fact, I have a meeting in ten minutes."

"Okay, just give me a minute," Susie said, taking a deep audible breath. "All right. Here's what happened. Remember how I told you Greg had asked Jessica and Scott to come down to Cedar Bay?"

"Yes, I thought they were going to arrive yesterday."

"They did. Both of them said they could only stay for the night because they had to get back home, Jessica for the girls, and Scott for business."

"Okay, that doesn't sound like any reason for you to be so upset."

"It wasn't. We took them to dinner at The Waterfront Restaurant, - like we always do. We drove the boat over to it. It's what happened at the restaurant," she said with a sob.

"Susie, this is eating up my time. What happened at the restaurant?"

"Well, Greg ordered swordfish…"

"Susie, I could care less what any of you ate. What happened that led to this call?"

"He's going to die, and he's going change his trust."

"What do you mean 'he's going die and he's going to change his trust'? Are you talking about Greg?"

"Of course I am. Who else would I be talking about?"

"Susie, I have no idea. First of all, why is he going to die? Is he sick?"

"He has pancreatic cancer, and his doctor says it's pretty much terminal."

"That's terrible. I wouldn't wish that on anyone," Kendra said noticing that Susie talked about Greg's death without any sounds of crying. "And what's this about his trust? People change their trusts all the time. What did he do, have some religious experience and decide he wants to give some money to charity?"

"I wish," Susie said with a sob. "He's going to leave me destitute. I get a lousy 10% of his estate. He's leaving almost all of it to Jessica.

Scott and I are getting chump change."

It was Kendra's turn to take a deep breath. If what Susie had just told her was true, and based on what she thought Greg's estate was worth, Susie would blow through that amount in a matter of months. She knew her sister had absolutely no common sense when it came to money. If it was in her bank account, she'd spend it.

What that meant was Susie would soon come running to her, broke, and expect Kendra to pick up the pieces just as she'd done countless times before Susie had managed to get Greg to marry her.

An icy cold feeling began at the base of Kendra's spine and started to work its way upward. There was no way she could allow Susie to live with her for even a day. She no longer had the patience to take care of a woman-child who refused to be financially responsible. No, she couldn't let that happen.

"Susie, are Jessica and Scott still there or did they go home?"

"They rented a car in Portland when they came down here. Scott drove it back, because Matt, Jessica's husband, picked her up in his plane."

"Has Greg actually changed his trust?"

"I don't think so, because he specifically said he was going to change it."

"So that means he hasn't actually met with an attorney to do it yet."

"I guess," Susie said. "You know I'm not real good with things like that."

Well I do, sister of mine, Kendra thought. *I certainly remember when I had to bail you out to the tune of $25,000 when you maxed out on your credit cards, and you couldn't even pay your rent. It was pay your debts and keep you in your apartment or have you come live with me. That was a no-brainer. No thanks.*

Been there, done that, and I'm not doing that again.

"Susie, I'm sure this will work out all right. I need a little time to think about it, but I want you to just relax. You'll be okay. Don't worry about anything."

"Well, I guess I'll have to come live with you, now that I'll be out on the street. I'll have to get rid of the Lexus, my jewelry, everything. Oh, Kendra, this is the worst day of my life. I'm just so glad I can rely on you to help me," Susie said.

Kendra was quiet for a moment thinking this could also end up being the worst day of her life, and then she said, "Susie, do you and Greg still go over to The Waterfront Restaurant several nights a week?"

"Yeah, we go there about five nights a week. You know I don't cook. I mean, cooking involves opening cans and things like that. I just know I'd break a nail. And they treat us really good," she said in an upbeat voice.

"Everyone knows us there. As a matter of fact, they even bring us our drinks as soon as we sit down. We don't even have to order. It's kind of like our home away from home."

"Susie, didn't you mention there's a waitress you like a lot there? Think you mentioned someone by the name of Mitzi?"

"Yeah, she's great. We used to ask for her, but now the owner knows that's who we want, so we're always seated at a table in her section."

"What's the restaurant's telephone number? Might be fun for me to send you flowers there for your upcoming birthday."

"Ooh, that would be spectacular. Everyone at the restaurant would probably sing Happy Birthday to me, like I was somebody really important. Here's the number. I know it by heart."

She gave Kendra the number and said, "Well, I have an appointment at the fitness center with my personal trainer. Life goes on, you know. Talk to you later," she said with a giggle.

After the call Kendra sat at her desk deciding what she was going to do. She looked at her finances and decided she could pay Mitzi $10,000. Greg was a nice guy, but there was no way Susie was going to come live with her. And after all, if he had to leave the world a little earlier than he'd planned, and he hadn't had a chance to see his attorney, Susie would get 1/3 of his estate, the original way he'd made out his trust.

She picked up her phone and moment later said, "I'd like to speak with one of your waitresses. I believe her name is Mitzi."

CHAPTER THREE

Johnny Larson looked at his calendar and saw that Susie Tuttle was scheduled for her regular training session with him at the fitness center in half an hour. He smiled, just thinking about her. They'd been having an affair for several months, and he was ready to take it to the next level.

She'd mentioned once that she'd refused to sign a premarital contract with her husband, Greg, when they got married, so he took that to mean that she'd get half of everything her husband had if she divorced him.

Just looking at her, you could tell that would be a lot. She drove a Lexus, she'd had a lot of work done, and she was dripping with expensive jewelry. It didn't take a rocket scientist to figure out that her husband had a lot of money, money that Johnny would like to get his hands on.

He'd deliberately become a fitness trainer with one goal in mind: to find a wealthy woman who could support him in the style to which he'd like to become accustomed. He'd struck gold when he found Susie Tuttle. It hadn't taken much to persuade her that she was the woman of his dreams. Now he just had to persuade her to divorce her husband.

"Good morning, Johnny. How are you today?" They always kept

their conversations very vanilla when other people were around. It was no secret around the fitness center that they were an item, but Johnny didn't think anyone knew the extent of their relationship.

He looked at her and said, "Mrs. Tuttle, is something wrong? It looks like you've been crying. Step over this way and you can tell me about it." He led her over to the side of the large exercise room, away from where people were working out, and indicated for her to sit down on a bench.

In a much different tone of voice, he said, "Susie, what's happened? I can tell you're really upset. Let me help."

"Oh, Johnny…"

"Go ahead, Susie. It won't help for you to keep it in."

"Greg's dying, and…"

Greg's dying, he thought. *This is the answer to my prayers. No Greg means no time-consuming divorce, and no Greg means Susie will get the money right away.*

"And he's changing his trust. He's only going to leave me 10%, not 1/3," she said as she started to cry again. "That won't be enough for me to live on for more than a few months."

Nor me, Johnny thought. *This is definitely not good news.*

"Has he changed his trust yet?" Johnny asked in what he hoped was a calm tone of voice.

"No, he's going to see his lawyer this week."

"So, Susie, that means if Greg died before he changes his trust, you'd still get 1/3 of his estate, is that right?"

"Yes, I guess so, but that's not going to happen. I don't know what I'm going to do."

"Susie, you trust me, don't you?"

"You know I do."

"Well, I might just be able to make everything right for you, and for us. Don't do anything for a few days, just trust in me. Will you do that for me?"

She looked at him and said, "Yes, Johnny, I will. What are you going to do?"

"Susie, don't you worry that pretty little head of yours. By the way, are you and Greg still eating at The Waterfront Restaurant almost every night? And are you still driving over in your inflatable dinghy when you do?"

"Oh, yes. It's about the only thing we do together anymore. I swear, if I didn't know better, I'd say he had a girlfriend for as little time as we spend together. But in answer to your question, yes, we drive the dinghy over there almost five nights a week. Usually we go on weeknights, because it gets really busy on the weekends with all the Portland people coming down to Cedar Bay."

This will work, Johnny thought. *I don't have much time, but I can make it work. Good thing I'm a kayaker. Won't be too hard to be in the water and watch them when they leave. Susie's told me she's good with boats, so I don't need to worry about her not being able to drive the boat when something happens to Greg.*

"Okay, pretty lady, everything is going to be just fine. The next few days may be a little rough, but you need to trust me. We'll be together very soon, I promise, and everything will be great. Now it's time to work out that beautiful body of yours. Follow me," he said as he stood up and walked over to a nearby treadmill.

CHAPTER FOUR

"Scott, you can't be serious," Nita, Scott's wife said angrily. "Too bad he's dying, but that's no excuse to cut us out of the money that should rightly go to us. What's he thinking? And to give it to that airhead sister of yours? I don't believe this."

"I'm serious, Nita, deadly serious. And not only did Dad say he was cutting my share back to 10%, he's also going to put in a stipulation that the trust has to be paid back the $100,000 I borrowed from him within forty-eight hours of his death, or I'll get nothing. He said he's going to see his attorney and make the changes sometime soon."

"Are you saying that he's not going to forgive that loan? I mean he's dying and he won't forgive a loan he made to us so we could buy some important household things? That's unforgiveable. I mean this whole thing is completely unacceptable to me. What are we going to do? We were going to talk to him in a couple of weeks or so about borrowing another $100,000, since we're up to our ears in debt as it is. Where does he think we can get the $100,000 to pay back his trust?"

"I have no idea. Think about it. With the changes to my share and to Susie's, not only will I forfeit the 10% bequest, but that amount will go to Jess. In other words, she'll get 90% of the estate rather than 80%, as she would if I could pay back the loan."

Nita's eyes bugged out. "Are you kidding me? I could understand, barely, I might add, if he deducted the $100,000 from your 10% share, but what I'm hearing is that if you, make that we, don't pay the trust back the $100,000, you get nothing from the trust. Is that what I'm hearing?"

"That's it, sweetheart. Pure and simple. Guess dear old dad is having the last laugh. But right now, the most important thing I have to do is figure out where I'm going to get $100,000 and quite frankly, the pickings are slim, real slim. I'm thinking of going to your dad and asking him."

"Don't waste your breath. Remember what happened last time. It was a disaster. We got a long lecture about how we didn't need half the things we were buying, with the bottom line being it would be a cold day in hell before he ever loaned us money for anything. No, that's not happening," Nita said.

"Yeah, I agree. Plus, I'm not so sure my ego is up to that kind of a battering again. Nita, I don't know what to do. On the plane ride back here, I looked through all my contacts on my phone and there's not a one I can get that kind of money from. Maybe a loan of $50 or $100, but $100,000, no way."

"Scott, who's the trustee of Greg's estate?"

"His friend, Mike Reynolds. He's the sheriff in Cedar Bay."

"Okay, so it's not Jess. Well, how about if you asked her for a loan of $100,000? From what I've heard from your mother, her husband's company is doing great. I'm sure she'd loan it to you, and you could pay the trust back with that money. Bingo! You could get your money, and even if it's only 10%, that's better than nothing."

"Nita, there is no way Jess would loan me $100,000 so I could get my 10% of Dad's estate. You know what a daddy's girl she is. She'd feel she owes it to Dad to do exactly what he wanted. And Dad was very clear last night about what he wanted done. And it was not for me to borrow $100,000 from my sister so I could get my 10%."

"Scott, how did Susie take the news that she was only getting 10%? Wasn't she getting 1/3, like you were, in his original trust? If so, she's in the same boat that you are."

"That's right. Her share is being reduced to 10% as well."

"Did he say why?" Nita asked.

"Yes. It was just one sentence. He told her that, as they both were well aware, their marriage had been one in name only for quite a while."

"You're kidding? That must have hurt. Wow. It's probably true, but still."

"Yeah, I agree. That was harsh, but I guess when you know you only have a short time to live, you kind of let the niceties of life go by. She started crying, but kept it pretty much under control."

"I bet she was crying because she was only getting 10% instead of 1/3 of his estate, not because he was dying."

"Nita, that's pretty harsh."

"May be, but from what I've seen of that blond bimbo, I'd be willing to bet it's the truth." She sat back and looked at her hands for a few moments, then she said, "Scott, those tears just might work to our advantage."

"What are you talking about? How?"

"Well, first of all Susie stands to lose as much money as we will, and that's a lot of money. The way Susie runs through money, she'll be lucky if the 10% amount lasts her a year."

"Yeah, well, guess what? Need I remind you that we're not too far behind her," Scott said.

"I know, but if you and she unite in a common cause, that cause being to save each of your 1/3 interest, you both would win."

"Nice thinking, sweetheart, but don't see how that's going to happen."

"Scott, what if you called Susie and told her if she could arrange for your father's death in the next few days, you'd both still get your 1/3 share of his estate, and if she was responsible for his death, you would even pay her 10% of whatever your take amounts to from the 1/3 amount you'll be receiving."

He looked at her wide-eyed. "Wait a minute, Nita. You want me to call Susie and tell her if she's responsible for murdering my dad in the next few days, that I'll pay her 10% of my take. Is that what I'm hearing you say?"

"Yes, that's exactly what I'm saying, my love. I'd bet anything that Susie is just as hungry for the 1/3 take as we are."

"I'm sure you're right about her being money hungry, but the devil is in the details. Like, how does she go about killing him without going to prison for murdering him?"

"You can drop the sarcastic tone of voice, Scott. Really, it wouldn't be all that difficult. Everyone knows they go to dinner at The Waterfront Restaurant almost every night, and everyone knows they have quite a few drinks when they go there.

"Well, what if your dad, at Susie's urging, had a couple more drinks than he usually does? What if he falls overboard and drowns? It would just be a tragic accident. Think about it. A man has too much to drink, falls overboard, and drowns. Happens all the time."

Scott was quiet for a long time and then said, "If you'd said something like this yesterday, before I went to Cedar Bay to see Dad, I would have said you were crazy. Now I think it's a very good plan. The only problem I have with it is Susie. She's kind of a loose cannon."

"Scott, if you present it to her as her only chance to get what she'd always expected to get out of the marriage, I bet she'd go along with it. Plus, it's nothing like using a gun, a knife, poison, or anything like that.

"She could make sure he's pretty drunk when they leave the restaurant. She could drive the boat like she usually does, and since he likes to stand up in the boat, you know how often we've seen him do that, it would be easy for her to fake an accident.

"Susie could do a sharp doughnut type of turn and make him fall overboard or simply push him out. Of course, she'd be hysterical afterwards. Who knows, she could even say he was driving, lost control of the boat, it started going around in circles, and he fell out. Really, it should be easy."

"I agree with you. It's plausible. There wouldn't be anything to link her to it other than a tragic boating accident happened on their way back home from the restaurant. In other words, there wouldn't be a smoking gun."

Nita picked up her phone and handed it to Scott. "Don't think about this, just do it. Call Susie right now. Your dad could be making the appointment to see the lawyer in the next day or so. Honestly, if time was ever of the essence, it's now."

"You're right, and it sure would solve all of our financial worries," he said as he took the phone from her.

"Yes, darling, it would. You don't have a choice. This is for us and our children."

CHAPTER FIVE

Kelly's son, Cash, was home on leave from his military duty in Afghanistan. He'd surprised Mike and Kelly by arranging for the three of them to take a trip to Hawaii while he was home on leave.

"There's the sign for long term parking," Cash said as Kelly, Mike, and he entered the Portland, Oregon airport complex. "See, right there. And there's a shuttle bus waiting to pick up passengers. Hopefully we can catch it, but even if we don't, we've got plenty of time before our flight leaves."

They got on the shuttle with their carry-on luggage, having decided the only things they really needed for their trip to Kauai were so lightweight, there was absolutely no point in checking their luggage. Mike and Cash had already called the golf shop at the hotel where they were staying and made arrangements to rent clubs.

Cash didn't have any golf clubs and Mike thought his would be an embarrassment at the resort where they were staying. He rather doubted any of the other guests there would be playing with Wal-Mart specials.

Security was a breeze that time of night, and they arrived at their gate forty-five minutes before they could board their plane. "Cash," Kelly said. "This may be the most exciting thing that's ever happened to me. You coming home from Afghanistan and then surprising us with this trip. I don't think it gets any better than this. I can't wait for the sun, the tropical sand, and having absolutely nothing to do."

"Wait a minute, Kelly. I'm feeling kind of like chopped liver here. I believe you told me that marrying me was the most exciting thing you'd ever done," Mike said with a grin.

"Sorry, Mike, but that was a while ago. This is today. I want to see hula dances, drink mai tais, and although I wanted to swim with the dolphins, from the research I did, no one offers that in Kauai."

"Well, Mom, I think we need to go snorkeling. We can go on one of those big boats that offer it, and who knows, maybe we'll get lucky and see some dolphins, but if not, we'll see a lot of other things that you'll never see in the waters of Cedar Bay."

"I just hope I can still play golf," Mike said. "I did pretty well when we were in Sonoma a few years ago, but I've only played a couple of times since then. Cash, I'd completely understand it if you decide to play at a different time than me and get with a group that will challenge you. Think I'll be playing catch up this entire week."

"Nope, you're stuck with me. I can't remember the last time the most important thing for me to do was decide whether I should play golf, have a mai tai, or walk from my room to the beach and take a dip in the ocean. Ahh, yes, I can already tell this is going to be a very difficult week for me."

"Mike, why don't you turn your phone off and not answer that call? The sheriff's station can do without you for a week," Kelly said as Mike's phone began to ring.

He looked down at it and said, "That's odd. It's Jessica, Greg's daughter. Wonder what she wants? I better take this call." He stood up and walked over to a quiet spot next to a nearby wall.

Kelly watched Mike as he talked on the phone. "Cash, something's wrong. Look at Mike, he's white. Watch our bags." She quickly stood up and hurried over to Mike who looked like he was in shock. Just as she got to him, he ended the call.

"Mike, what's wrong? Is Jessica all right?"

"Physically, yes, emotionally, no. Greg and Susie were going home from The Waterside Restaurant tonight. Greg fell out of their inflatable boat and drowned. The Coast Guard had to pull him out of the water. They don't know what happened to him."

"Oh, no! How is Jessica doing?"

"As well as can be expected. She's flying up in Mark's plane tomorrow. His parents are going to watch their children."

"What about Scott and Susie? How are they doing?"

"I don't know. Jess said that Susie's sister is on her way to Cedar Bay, and Scott will arrive tomorrow. Kelly, I can't leave for our vacation. I told you the terms of the trust, and I don't know if Greg was able to have a new one drawn up or not. You and Cash go on without me. Maybe I'll be able to get over there in a couple of days, but I need to be in Cedar Bay right now. I hope you understand."

Cash had been watching the exchange and walked over to them, hearing the last few words Mike had said. "What's happening, Mike?"

Mike quickly told him. Cash immediately said, "We're going back to Cedar Bay with you. I'll cancel the hotel, and give me one minute to see if I can do something about our airline tickets. Airlines often have a policy concerning deaths." He turned and hurried over to the counter next to the boarding gate.

Several minutes later he returned and said, "We're in luck. I told them what had happened, that it was your closest friend, and that the decedent's daughter was your goddaughter. The airline is giving us a full refund. Let's get the car, and tell me what I can do to help."

"Oh, Cash. This is part of your leave, and you won't be able to get more for quite a while. Why don't you go and just enjoy Kauai on your own? I need to stay with Mike. I hope you understand," Kelly said.

"Of course I do, Mom, but I want to be here to help, however I can. Hey, I'm part of the family, too. I'm sure there's something I'll be able to do. Right now we need to get the car. I'll drive. It's okay, we'll go to Hawaii in a few months. Actually, I have so much leave built up, I'm sure I can take some time off in a few months, and we can go once this is all settled."

"Cash, thank you," Mike said. "I'm so sorry to be the one who has to ruin our trip, but this is something I have to do. I hope you understand."

"Mike, I don't talk about it much, but there's a lot I've had to do in the past couple of years for friends of mine who were killed while we were in Afghanistan. Yeah, I'm pretty familiar with having to do what's right, and you're doing what's right."

CHAPTER SIX

Cash drove towards Cedar Bay while Mike made phone calls. The first call he made was to his number one deputy, Josh.

"Josh, it's Sheriff Reynolds. Understand there was a drowning in the bay tonight. Tell me about it. By the way, I'm headed back to Cedar Bay as we speak. I'm not going on vacation. I'll be at the station tomorrow, but I want to hear what happened."

"Sheriff, we got a call from someone who was in a boat in the bay and saw a man go overboard from a small inflatable dinghy. He said the boat kept going around in circles after the man fell overboard. I called the Coast Guard, and they were on the scene in less than five minutes. I immediately went there. When I got there, they had floodlights focused on the bay, trying to find the man. They finally found him and pulled him out of the water, but it was too late. He was dead."

"I understand the decedent was Greg Tuttle."

"Yes, sir. His widow, her name is Susie Tuttle, said her husband was a friend of yours. She was pulled out of the water by some neighbors, and other than a few scratches, she's fine physically, but emotionally not so good."

"Yes, Greg was my best friend. Why did they have to pull her out of the water? What happened to his inflatable?"

"His wife said he was driving the boat, lost control, and it started going around in circles. That was when he fell out of it. She was up in front and couldn't do anything to stop it when it headed for a dock and crashed into one of their neighbor's boats. She was thrown out of the boat and into the bay.

"With the lights and commotion, the owners of the boat she crashed into were already out on the dock. They threw her a flotation pillow, pulled her over to the dock, and helped her up."

"You said the inflatable hit the guy's boat. I'm assuming there was damage to both boats."

"Yes, sir. The boat the inflatable hit really took a beating. It was one of those old boats with a lot of wood, think it's teak, anyway, it's got a huge hole in the rear transom. The owner said he was going to take it to Jack's Marine Repair tomorrow and have them fix it.

"Evidently he's planning on taking it on a trip in a couple of weeks and he needs it fixed, like yesterday. Said it's an annual family thing. His kids and grandkids come up every year and spend a week on the boat. It's a pretty big boat."

"From everything I'm hearing sounds like Greg just fell overboard and drowned. This is the lawman in me, Josh, any hint there was more to it than just an accident?"

"Not at this point, Sheriff. The county coroner just happened to be in Cedar Bay visiting his in-laws and had the coroner's van with him. He took the body back to the county morgue. He said he'd do an autopsy tomorrow to check for drugs or anything else. Hate to say it, but since they were coming from The Waterfront Restaurant, be willing to bet your friend Greg's blood alcohol was pretty high. Maybe that's what caused him to fall out of the boat, you know, lost his balance."

"Could be, but I've known Greg for a long time, and while he enjoys his Scotch, I've never seen him intoxicated. He's a big man, and he can handle a lot of alcohol. How's his wife doing?"

"When I left her, not all that well. She had two friends at the house with her and she was hysterical, drinking wine, and saying it was all her fault, that she should have done something to save Greg. One of her friends told her she'd had enough wine and took her glass away from her. Under the circumstances, can't say I blame the widow. If it was me, might have done the same thing."

"Yeah, this has to be hard on her. I won't be home until about 3:00 a.m., but I'll go over there tomorrow and see what I can do. Call me if you find out anything else," Mike said as he ended the call.

"Thanks for putting it on speakerphone, Mike. Saves you the trouble of having to repeat everything to us. Want me to go to Susie's with you tomorrow?" Kelly asked, putting her hand on his arm, silently indicating that she knew how hard this was for him.

"No, I know Susie wasn't one of your favorite people, and quite frankly, not one of mine either, but as trustee of Greg's trust, I'm going to have to deal with her, so I might as well make it as smooth as possible. I'll get some sleep and go over there a little later tomorrow."

"When do you expect Jess and Scott will arrive?"

"When I talked to Jess, she said they'd be at the house around 1:00 or so. Scott's flying into Portland and will arrive about the same time. Actually, this will give me a chance to talk to Lem Bates and see if anything has been done about Greg's trust. I told you what he was planning to do, but whether or not he'd gotten around to it, I have no way of knowing."

"Mike, I'd like to go with you, if you don't mind," Cash said. "I've never met Susie, so my being there shouldn't push anybody's buttons. Plus, through you, I know Jess and Scott, and I'd like to give them my condolences. And maybe if I'm there, this Susie won't fall apart as easily as she might if it was just you."

"Thanks, Cash, I'll take you up on that, and you might be right about Susie. As you can tell, I'm dreading it. If Greg did change his trust, this could get very ugly, and since Jess and Scott are only going to be here for a day or so, I need to tell them what's going to happen with the trust."

"Why only a day, Mike?" Kelly asked. "Are they not going to have a funeral or anything for him."

"No. Greg was always adamant that he wanted to be cremated and have his ashes scattered over the ocean by the funeral home, not by his family. Ever since I've known him, that's what he'd always say when the subject of death came up. Jess mentioned it to me as well. There will be no service of any kind."

"I don't know, Mike," Kelly said. "It's been my experience that people need some closure when something like this happens. When there's no service or celebration of life or anything else, it seems a little cold. If the three of them would like to have a little gathering at the house, I'd be happy to cater it at no charge. Please tell them that."

"I will, but I'd bet Jess, who I think is the strongest of the three, would want to honor her dad's wishes and will say no thanks. Anyway, I'm sure we'll be talking of little else for the next few days. Right now, I'm just glad to see our house coming into view, and I'm ready for bed. As much as I love our dogs, I'm kind of glad they're at the kennel tonight."

"Don't worry about them," Kelly said. "I'll pick them up tomorrow. Cash, thanks for driving. Tomorrow should be interesting."

CHAPTER SEVEN

"Mornin', Roxie," Kelly said to her coffee shop manager after she'd placed a call to her. Guess what? I'm back and will be in later today after I pick up the dogs at the kennel. How's everything going?"

"Absolutely fine, and I'm guessing you didn't go to Hawaii because of Greg Tuttle's death, right? I know he was a very close friend of Mike's. How's Mike doing?"

"He's taking it well. He and Greg met about a week ago and Greg told him he had terminal cancer, so as tragic as his death is, in some ways Mike was already prepared for it. What he isn't looking forward to is the drama that always goes along with this type of death, and knowing what the widow is going to be like."

"Yeah, I heard she took it real hard. Shannon Michaels was in here early on this morning. Said she needed a good breakfast and a lot of coffee because she'd just left Susie's house after staying with her until her sister arrived this morning."

"This town amazes me. I mean the poor guy just died last night and already it's all over town."

"Yeah, well isn't that what living in a small town is all about? Everybody knows everybody else's business and everything about them."

"Yes. There are good sides and bad sides to living in a small town, and that just might be the bad side. What did she say about Susie?"

"Said she was hysterical and more or less out of control. I guess she was drinking a lot of wine, which just made it worse. Shannon said she remembered once that Susie told her Doc Burkham had given her some sleeping pills because she'd been having trouble sleeping. Shannon found them and gave her one, even though the bottle said to take two. She was afraid that Susie might have had too much to drink and mixing a full dose of sleeping pills with wine might cause a fresh set of problems."

"Mike talked to his deputy last night and he said she kept saying it was all her fault. Did Shannon say anything about that?"

"She sure did. Shannon and Jodie, her friend from the fitness center, tried to tell her that it was just an accident and that it wasn't her fault. I don't remember what it's called, but I think I've read that when someone dies, the survivor often feels guilty."

"I'm guessing that's what she's feeling. I mean when someone falls out of a boat, there's not much you can do, and particularly with a guy as big as Greg. There was no way she could have pulled him back into the boat, even if she had found him."

"Well, it certainly was a tragedy. Earlier I said I'd be in today, but since you weren't planning on me being there anyway, I think I better be available in case Mike needs me. Plus, Cash is ending his leave because of this and is going back to Afghanistan. I'd like to spend a little time with him, and I need to get some groceries. Okay with you?"

"Of course, take as long as you need. We're perfectly capable of keeping Kelly's Koffee Shop up and running for as long as you need to be gone. If you decide not to come in today, no big deal."

"Thanks, Roxie. I don't know what I'd do without you. Talk to you later."

*****

After stocking up at the grocery store, going to the post office to tell them to resume delivery of their mail, and taking care of numerous other things that were on her to-do list, Kelly walked into the Doggie Love Kennel where she always boarded her dogs. Rebel, a boxer, Lady, a yellow lab, and Skyy, a German Shepherd, happily went there whenever Mike and Kelly needed to leave town for a few days.

Kelly's solving of the kennel owner's murder a few years back had made her a hero in the eyes of the kennel personnel. Even the new ones had heard about her, so making an appointment for her dogs was never a problem.

"Hello, Mrs. Reynolds, I hope the reason you're back so early isn't because of a problem. We're sorry your dogs are leaving early, because they're our favorites. Oops, I shouldn't have said that. Please don't tell the owners. We're supposed to like all the dogs equally, but you'd have to be a real non-dog lover not to get attached to Rebel, Lady, and Skyy."

"As a matter-of-fact we did have to come back early because of a problem, although that isn't quite the correct word to use. My husband's closest friend died in a freak boating accident. We never made it out of the airport," Kelly said.

The young woman had a funny look on her face which Kelly didn't understand.

"I'm sorry, but I can't help but notice the expression on your face. Do you know something about this?"

The girl looked down at her hands and then at the clock on the opposite wall. "Mrs. Reynolds, I'll go get the dogs for you. Then I need to check on the kennels. I'll be right back."

"No, wait. Please tell me what you know about this. I can see it on your face and hear it in your voice. There's something else, isn't there? I promise whatever you tell me won't go any further," Kelly said. "Please, it could be important."

"All right. My mother's best friend is Rae Ann Burns. She came over to our house early this morning in tears, and I couldn't help but overhear their conversation when I was getting ready to come here."

"I don't think I know her. Does she live here in Cedar Bay?"

"No, she lives in Ninac, where we live. She was crying because Greg Tuttle died."

"Greg was retired. How did she know him?" Kelly asked with a sick feeling growing in her stomach.

"Please don't judge Rae Ann. She's really nice. I guess she's been in a bad marriage for a long time. As a matter of fact, she served her husband with divorce papers recently."

"And was this because of her relationship with Greg?" Kelly asked.

The young woman nodded her head up and down. "From what I overheard, I would say yes. To answer your question, she met him on the internet on some dating site. She told Mom he was the one who had gotten in touch with her. She said he'd stopped calling her, but she knew it was because of his wife. Greg had told her he loved her. She didn't understand what had happened."

"Well, I know Greg's marriage wasn't the best, but I didn't know about that. My husband was his closest friend. Maybe he knew. Did Rae Ann say anything else?"

"Not really. My mom got her some coffee and she seemed better after that."

"Do you think her relationship with Greg was a surprise to your mom or do you think she knew about it?"

"I'm sure from the things my mother was saying that she didn't know about it. As a matter of fact, Rae Ann said she'd never told anyone about it, because both she and Mr. Tuttle were married. I mean, I know those things happen, but when the love of your life, and that's what she called him, dies in a freak boating accident, that's pretty heavy."

"Yes, it is."

"Do you think she killed him?"

"Who?" Kelly asked

"His wife. Rae Ann thinks she did."

"Why would she think that?" Kelly asked. "From what I know, he fell out of his boat, and it was a tragic accident."

"Rae Ann said he and his wife had a very bad marriage. She's sure that his wife found out about the relationship and made it look like he fell overboard."

Kelly was quiet for several moments and then said, "I have no idea. In addition to being Greg's best friend, my husband is the sheriff, so I'm sure he'll investigate, as he would any other death under those circumstances."

"I hope for Rae Ann's sake he finds out something. She was pretty devastated. Well, I've talked enough. Time to get your dogs. Back in a minute," she said, stepping out from behind the counter and walking through a door that led to the kennels.

A moment later three dogs had surrounded Kelly and were yipping with delight at seeing her. She always had to laugh at their reaction when she returned from somewhere, even if it was only getting the mail.

If they could speak, she knew they'd be saying, "Thank heavens you're back. I thought I'd never see you again."

"Okay guys, time to go home. This was a short stay."

She turned to the young woman and said, "Thanks for telling me. I appreciate your confidence, and as tragic as it is, I'm sure Mike will find out whatever there is to be found out."

She opened the door, waved to the young woman, and managed to get three very excited dogs into her minivan.

CHAPTER EIGHT

As soon as Kelly and the dogs got home, she opened the back door for them. They ran in and out, checking every nook and cranny of the house and yard to make sure nothing had changed during their absence.

Kelly unloaded the groceries and began getting ready for dinner, not sure whether Cash and Mike would be starving or feeling like they couldn't eat after what was probably a very emotional afternoon.

She decided to fix a mixed green salad with seared ahi tuna, melons and fruit in a sweet yogurt sauce, warm sourdough bread, and caramel pecan turtle brownies that she wanted to try with a new ingredient she'd been told about by Roxie.

Roxie had told her a couple of weeks earlier that when she was a young girl her mother would put a can of condensed milk in boiling water. She'd let it simmer for around three hours or so and when the can was opened after it had cooled, it had become a creamy caramel, similar to dulce de leche. She was a little sketchy on how long her mother cooked it, but said it didn't matter because a company now sold it just like what she'd had as a child.

Kelly had bought a can before they'd left for Hawaii and tried it on ice cream, which she thought was delicious. For dessert this evening, she intended to spread it on the brownies and make them so irresistible it couldn't help but take Cash and Mike's thoughts off of what she was sure had been a very difficult meeting.

She spent the next hour prepping dinner, checking her email, and getting her mental attitude geared to Cedar Bay, rather than on the beach at Kauai, where it had been for the last few days.

She heard Mike's car pull into the garage, and as usual, the dogs raced to the door that led to the garage, ready to greet him and be petted. Having Cash here was an added bonus for them. A moment later she heard Mike and Cash greet the dogs.

"Hey Mom, got good stuff for dinner?"

"You doubt?" Kelly replied with a smile.

"Well, I hope so. Think Mike and I could both use a glass of wine after our afternoon. I'll get it."

"That bad, huh?" she asked.

"Yep. I'll let Mike tell you all about it. Poor guy really took a beating, but he held up beautifully. I was proud of him."

"I'm glad you were with him," Kelly responded with an appreciative smile.

"So am I," Cash said.

When Mike entered the kitchen a few moments later he took the glass of wine Cash handed him and took a long drink. "Thanks, Cash. I needed that more than I knew. What a nightmare," he said, raking his fingers through his hair.

"Want to tell me about it, or want to wait a while? I'm fine with either," Kelly said as she used her melon scoop to make the fruit bowls.

"I think I'd like to talk about it. I just don't know where to start.

I'm sure Greg thought he'd have time to get everyone around to his way of thinking before he died. Matter of fact, he kind of had a blind eye to that kind of thing. He always thought he could bring people around to his way of thinking if he kept at them long enough, but he seriously miscalculated this one."

"Did you have a chance to meet with Greg's attorney, Lem, before you went to Susie's house?"

"Yes. I called him just after you left this morning and was able to get an appointment right away. In some ways I was hoping that Greg hadn't had a chance to change his trust, because I knew it would make my job easier. I wouldn't have to deal with the additional drama of the trust change. Greg's untimely death was drama enough."

"And from what you're saying, I'm taking it that he did change his trust."

"Yes. Ironically, he signed the amended trust yesterday morning. Talk about coincidence. What if he'd made the appointment for today? Susie, Jess, and Scott's lives would be entirely different."

"Mike," Cash said. "I like Lem. I kind of vaguely remember him, although I don't know from what, but I thought he handled everything very professionally. I particularly thought it was a class act for him to insist he go to Susie's house with us to tell them in person the terms of the trust."

"Lem went with you?" Kelly said in a surprised voice. "I've never known him to do anything like that, but then again, this is a pretty unusual situation."

"Yes, we drove in separate cars and he met us there. And the way it turned out, I'm really glad."

"Mike, hold the thought. I don't know about you, but the dogs are driving me nuts. They're about an hour past their usual dinner time, and I don't think they're going to let up until they're fed. Back in a minute."

CHAPTER NINE

"There," Kelly said as she returned from the laundry room where she fed the dogs. "That should hold them for a while. I'm going to join you in a glass of wine and then let's go into the great room where we can be more comfortable while you tell me what happened."

A few minutes later, she turned to Mike and said, "Okay, dinner can hold for as long as needed. I want to hear all about what happened."

"We arrived and found Susie, Jess, Scott, and Susie's sister, Kendra, all gathered at Susie's home. And I want to tell you, her sister Kendra is a real piece of work. Okay back to what happened."

Cash interrupted him. "First of all, Scott and Jess were surprised to see me, and I can't blame them. I expressed my condolences, gave them each a hug, and said I would be leaving tomorrow…"

"Tomorrow? Oh, Cash, I didn't know that," Kelly said. "Can't you stay longer?"

"I wish I could. I was able to contact my commanding officer today, and he said if I wanted to take some leave in a few months, I'd better get back there now. Since I'm the second in command, I know he needs me. I rented a car today, and I can drop it off at the Portland airport tomorrow. I didn't want you to have to make a four-hour round trip just to see me off."

"Well, that was very thoughtful of you, but completely unnecessary. Nothing is an inconvenience when it comes to you, except that I don't get to see you enough," Kelly said.

"Just a few months, Mom, and we'll be sitting on the beach in Kauai with a mai-tai. Promise."

"I'm going to hold you to that. Okay, back to what happened."

"After all the condolences and similar things were said…"

"Mike, had you told Susie and the group that Lem was going to come with you to the meeting?"

"No. After I heard what had happened about the trust being signed, I was afraid if they'd had time to prepare themselves by wondering if it had been rewritten, it might really make things uncomfortable for Lem. In retrospect, I'm not so sure I did the right thing."

"Why?" Kelly asked.

"We all sat down in the living room. I remember looking out at the bay and thinking this might be the last calm moment in my relationship with them, and I was right. I introduced Lem and told them that he wanted to discuss the terms of Greg's trust with them. I asked them if they were comfortable with Kendra being there, since she was not one of the trust beneficiaries."

"I don't know if you noticed, Mike, but when you said that I happened to be looking at Kendra, and she was furious you'd even suggest she should be excluded from the conversation. Her eyes were on fire and her lips were in the grimmest line I've seen in a while," Cash said.

"No, I was more focused on Susie, Scott, and Jess. Susie spoke up immediately and said that her sister would be staying to hear what

Lem had to say. As ditzy as Susie is, she really pulled out a commanding voice indicating that Kendra was going to stay. Neither Scott nor Jess said a word, so Kendra stayed."

"Mike, keep talking," Cash said. "Give me your glass, and I'll get us a refill. After the afternoon we've had, I don't think anyone would begrudge us a second glass of wine." Mike held out his glass and Cash walked into the kitchen to get more wine for them.

"After that, I told them Lem would read the terms of the trust, and he did."

"And then?"

"Well, that's when it got ugly. Susie became hysterical, her sister kept saying that Greg had promised Susie she'd get a third of his estate and he'd personally told her that several times when she'd come to visit. She said Susie would sue the trust. Scott pretty much said the same thing. He said his father had always told him that when he died, the $100,000 loan Greg had made to him would be forgiven. He couldn't believe he had to re-pay it to the trust before he'd get his share."

"Lem responded to that by reading them the clause in the trust that says if any of the trust beneficiaries sues the trust, such a lawsuit will be deemed cause for them to be disinherited entirely and entitled to nothing."

"Sounds like Greg thought of everything. Mike, did the trust specify how much time Scott had to pay his loan back?" Kelly asked.

"I can answer that, Mom," Cash said, walking back into the room and handing a glass of wine to Mike. "According to the trust, Scott has forty-eight hours from the time of Greg's death, so the clock is ticking."

"Yes, Kelly," Mike said. "That was very specifically addressed in Greg's trust. Scott was beyond mad. I'd say he was more in a panic mode. He told his sister she'd have to loan him the money so he could pay back the trust and then he'd pay her when he received his share of the trust."

"Wow, he must really be desperate. What did Jess say?"

"Poor Jess. I think she was the only one, along with me, who was truly mourning Greg's death. You could tell just by looking at her that she was doing everything she could just to get through the day, much less have to deal with all of the emotions."

"Given that situation, are Jess and Scott going to drive back to Portland together?"

"No, Jess' husband is flying into Cedar Bay this afternoon to pick her up."

"We got sidetracked. What did she say in response to Scott asking for money?" Kelly asked.

"I have to tell you, Mom, I was really impressed by her answer," Cash said. "She looked at her brother and at Susie and said, 'This is my father's trust, not yours, and I will do nothing to get in the way of what he wanted. Mike is the trustee of the trust, and I know he will do what my father wanted. For me, this discussion is over.'"

"My heart just goes out to her," Mike said. "Susie went nuts. She said, 'I always knew you were just a money-grubbing little...' That's when I told her in my best sheriff's manner that there would be none of that kind of talk. Then she went on and said she knew that Jess was behind Greg's decision to change the terms of his trust. She said she was sure all the calls and text messages that Greg had sent and received lately had been from Jess about changing the trust to cut Scott and Susie out, or at least drastically reduce the amount of their share."

"Poor Jess. It would be hard enough to have the father you adored die in such a tragic way, but then to have your brother and step-mother be so awful?" Kelly said. "Poor thing. What did she do when you left? Talk about throwing fresh meat to a bunch of hungry animals."

"We didn't leave her there. We took her to the airport and waited for her husband to fly in and pick her up," Cash said.

"I'm glad you did. What did she have to say while you were waiting for her husband?"

"She told me she would not have anything to do with Susie ever again. Jess said she'd been a problem ever since she'd married Greg. Evidently she really likes her wine and several times when they visited Jess' family, her drinking caused some real problems.

"She told me she was sure her father wanted to divorce her, but his other two divorces had cost him so much money, he felt he was too old to go through it again."

"Did you ask what she was going to do about Scott?"

"I did, and she said Scott either pays the money he owes the trust by the time it's due, or he gets nothing. That's the way Greg wanted it. She said her father had made excuses and financially carried Scott for a long time. She thinks he just got fed up with being an ATM machine for Scott."

"That poor young woman. She's not only lost her dad, she's probably lost her brother as well."

"I agree, Mom, but that poor young woman, as you refer to her, is going to be worth several million dollars in the near future. That kind of money can make up for a lot of things, like brothers who have always been on the take from daddy."

"I suppose you're right," Kelly said. "Now what?"

"According to Lem, we wait out the forty-eight hours and see if Scott can get the money together to pay back the trust. Either way, in forty-eight hours, we start the formal trust administration proceedings. I'll have to make a list of the assets and determine what needs to be sold. If Jess wants to keep the house, there's actually enough money in a couple of Greg's bank accounts to pay off both Susie and Scott. Once all this emotional stuff is over, or at least calms down, taking care of the financial stuff should be fairly easy."

"Was there any talk about how Greg fell in the ocean?"

"No, ironically there wasn't. I had thought they'd be very anxious to find out if he'd had a heart attack or something else, but it was never brought up when we were all together. When we were waiting for Jess' husband to fly in, she asked me to let her know when the autopsy was completed, because she had some questions about his death."

"Like what?" Kelly asked.

"She didn't say, but taking off my hat as trustee of the trust and putting on my sheriff's hat, I need to ask some questions and make sure that his death was an accidental drowning. I'll start on that tomorrow."

"Okay, think with that we need to go in the kitchen. Everything is ready for dinner with the exception of flash frying the tuna, and that only takes a couple of minutes. Meet you in there," Kelly said as she stood up and walked towards the kitchen.

CHAPTER TEN

The next morning Kelly leaned over Mike and gave him a kiss. "Wake up, sleepyhead. Cash is leaving early this morning, and I want to make him some cinnamon rolls he can eat while he's driving. I know he said he didn't want a sit-down breakfast, because he was anxious to get going, but this will only take me a few minutes. Why don't you take a quick shower, and I'll meet you in the kitchen?"

Thirty minutes later, Cash walked into the kitchen, duffel bag in hand and dressed in military fatigues. "Morning, sweetheart," Kelly said. "Ready for a long couple of days of travel?"

"No, not really. It's kind of a necessary evil. Fortunately, I've always been able to sleep when I'm flying, and I have a couple of good books on my iPad, so I'm good to go. Plus, you'd be amazed how many people come up to me and thank me for my service to our country. It's kind of heartwarming."

"I always do the same thing when I'm traveling if I see a person who's in the military. I'll thank them for their service, and I mean it just as much as the people who say it to you. I know you said you didn't want a sit-down breakfast, but I made some cinnamon rolls for you, and here's a travel cup of coffee. You can just toss it when you get to the car rental return. I've got plenty," she said as she handed him a sack of rolls and his cup of coffee.

"Mom, I don't do real well with goodbyes as you know, so here's a kiss and see you in a couple of months on our way to Kauai." He kissed her and put the arm not holding the sack around her, pulling her in for a long hug.

"You're not getting out of here without a hug from me, too," Mike said as he gave Cash a big manly hug.

"Mike, let me know what happens with this whole Greg Tuttle thing. Having been on the ground floor of it, I'm really curious as to what's going to happen."

"Will do, but trust me, you're no more curious than I am. Now get out of here. The longer you wait, the more the traffic will build up. Stay safe and see you in a couple of months."

"Love you both," Cash said. He bent down to give each of the dogs a pat on their heads, then he stood up, slung his duffel bag over his shoulder, saluted them, and walked out to his car. All three dogs ran to the window and whimpered as they watched him back out of the driveway.

"I can't watch him leave," Kelly said. "I'm always afraid it will be the last time I'll ever see him." Tears were streaming down her face. She walked over to Mike who wrapped his arms around her.

"Kelly, Cash is as street smart as anyone can be. Plus, as second in command, he's not in as much danger as he used to be. I'm not saying he's not in danger, I just don't think he's in as much danger. He'll be fine. Just a couple more months and we'll be heading to Hawaii with him."

He released her and walked over to a Kleenex box on the kitchen counter. "Dry your tears," he said, handing her a tissue. "You've done a wonderful job raising him, and he'll be just fine. Now, what's on your agenda for today?"

"I'm going into the coffee shop and work today. Roxie is the best ever for overseeing things when I'm gone, but it's kind of like 'the buck stops here.' I can't ask her to make decisions that I should be making. Plus, I'm always nervous about how it's going when I'm not there, so this will relieve me. And you?" she asked.

"I want to find out how much Greg had to drink at the restaurant. Maybe that, along with being ill, caused him to fall out of the boat. I thought I'd do that this afternoon. While I was at Susie's yesterday, I went into Greg's office and went through his files. I brought a lot of them home, thinking they could probably help me start to determine the nature and extent of his assets."

"I noticed a bunch of files on your desk. So that's what they are."

"Yes. I'm hoping that the coroner will have his report finished sometime today. I still wonder if Greg had a heart attack, and that's why he fell out of the boat. The autopsy should show that."

"Sounds like you're really troubled by him falling out of the boat."

"I am, Kelly. He was a very experienced boatman and they'd made the run between their dock and The Waterfront Restaurant hundreds of times. According to Josh, it didn't seem that there was anything in the water the boat could have hit, so falling out of the boat? It just doesn't fit with Greg's boating experience.

"I'm also curious about the woman, Rae Ann. She's the woman Greg told me about when we had a drink at The Waterfront. She's the same woman you told me about after dinner last night. Greg asked me to tell her he loved her after he died. I don't know if it will help her to know Greg's true feelings, but I'd feel better about it."

"Well, as distraught as the young woman at the kennel told me she was, I definitely think she would want to hear it. May be another tough meeting for you. Are you going into the station today?"

"I thought about it, but I'm officially still on vacation, so think I'll use today to sift through those files of Greg's as well. Anyway, I'll see you tonight. I can tell you're anxious to get going."

"I am and before you leave, let the dogs out one last time."

"Will do and I love you."

CHAPTER ELEVEN

Mike spent the morning going through the files he'd taken with him from Greg's house. By noon, he had a rough estimate of what Greg's estate was worth, which was a lot more than he'd thought.

There was the house in Cedar Bay, which many people said was probably the most desirable house in the city. It was situated on the bay with a fifty-foot dock which a large boat could side-tie to, a rarity for the homes on the bay. Not only did that make the home desirable, but so did the floor-to-ceiling windows in the rear of the house that looked out at the bay and the outside entertainment area which was equipped with a barbecue, smoker, covered patio, and essentially a complete kitchen.

Greg's father had bought a house in Palm Springs, California, as a get-away when he'd taken up golf many years ago. It had been the first one built on a golf course which had become one of the premier retirement communities in the desert. It was worth several million dollars, and if the trust beneficiaries decided to list it for sale, it would probably be an easy sale.

Additionally, there was Greg's big boat, several checking accounts, stocks, money market accounts, a gun collection, and antiques that Greg had inherited when his parents had died. Altogether, Mike determined that Greg's estate was going to be worth around seven or eight million dollars.

Mike sat back in his chair thinking about the trust beneficiaries. Depending on whether or not Scott was able to pay the trust back by tomorrow, Jess would inherit either 80% or 90% of the trust estate. And Susie's 10% of the trust, approximately $800,000, was a lot less than it would have been if Greg had not been able to get to Lem's office to sign the revisions to his trust. There was quite a difference between eight hundred thousand dollars and two and a half million dollars.

No wonder Scott and Susie were upset. It was a pretty natural reaction, Mike thought. *If it were me, I'd probably feel the same way.*

Just as he was finishing his review of the trust assets, his phone rang and he saw Jessica's name on the monitor. "Good morning, Jess. I trust you got home safe and sound and your girls were glad to see you."

"Yes, everyone was glad I was back including our bulldog puppy, Bully," she said.

"Seriously, Jess? A bulldog puppy named Bully? I thought you were a lot more creative than that," Mike said jokingly.

"Mike, if you met Bully, you'd think it was a perfect name for him. Trust me on this one."

"I'll look forward to it. To change the subject, how are you doing?"

"I'm still hurting, but I guess I better get used to it. Dad's not coming back," she said with a catch in her voice.

"Jess, I wish I could tell you that he was coming back, but we both know that's not going to happen. And yes, you will have to get used to it. Over the years as sheriff, I've had to witness a lot of people dealing with a loved one's death. Your grief will never completely go away, but I will tell you, trite as it sounds, that with time, it will get easier. I know that seems impossible now, but I promise, it truly will get easier."

"I know you're right, Mike, but that's a concept I'm having a hard time wrapping my head around right now. Anyway, that's not why I called."

"Jess, just know I'm here for you. You can call me any time. Please remember that."

"I will. Thanks. Mike, Scott must have called me twenty times last night and this morning, plus he's sent me I don't know how many emails and texts. They all say pretty much the same thing, that he can backdate a check and put it into the account, so he can technically meet the terms of the trust. He's says that if I don't loan him the $100,000, it will cost him about $800,000. The last few messages have been really nasty, calling me all kinds of names."

"Oh honey, I'm so sorry. That's unforgiveable. You sure don't need that right now. Block him on your phone and your computer. If he can't come up with the money, that's his problem, not yours. Your father was pretty sure he wouldn't be able to, but wanted to give him two days of grace, in case Scott had sent the money by mail, but it just hadn't reached him before he died."

"Yes, it looks like he won't be getting anything from the trust, and in that case, I'll be getting 90% of it, which is a lot of money. You know that my husband, Mark, is very successful, so I really don't even need the money."

"Yes, I know, but your father wanted you to have it, because he told me his marriage was nothing more than in name only, and his son was a failure. You were the one bright light for him."

Jessica sighed. "I know, and I'll do what my father wanted done per the terms of his trust. However, I've been thinking. Did Dad ever tell you about a woman named Rae Ann Burns?"

"Yes, he mentioned her name to me once. Actually it was the last time I saw him. He said that he'd found the love of his life, but it was too late because of his cancer diagnosis. Do you know if that's her?

"I found out about her a few months ago when we were talking about things we regretted and he mentioned that he hoped I wouldn't think any of the less of him for telling me what he was about to reveal to me. You know how close we were."

"I sure do. What did he tell you?"

"He told me he'd met a woman on a dating site and they'd been seeing each other for several months. He said he wasn't very proud of having an affair when he was married, but that he'd fallen in love with her. I didn't have a chance to ask him if she knew he had cancer at dinner the other night because Susie was there, but I can't stop thinking about her. I wonder if she knows."

"Coincidentally, just yesterday, Kelly had a conversation with a young woman at the kennel where we board our dogs. Here's what she told Kelly." He related what Kelly had told him the night before about Rae Ann.

"Mike, it sounds like Rae Ann didn't know that Dad had cancer. At least not when she talked to that woman's mother."

"Yes, I agree. I've thought about her, too. Actually, your father wanted me to talk to her."

"If you would go see her and tell her about Dad's cancer, I'd consider it a favor. I know Dad loved her and I think she needs to know that. Also, Mike, and I know some people would say this is crazy, but I want to give her $100,000 out of my proceeds from the trust. No one else needs to know about it but you, Rae Ann, and me. I think Dad would have wanted her to have something, but couldn't do it because of Susie."

"That's very generous of you, Jess. Are you sure about this?"

"Yes, if she made my father happy, then she should be compensated for it. I'm just sorry Susie has to get anything, but if she was cut out of the trust, knowing her, she'd probably sink the boat or set fire to the house. I always thought she was a little to the left of normal. I know she was great arm candy for dad, but I have a feeling that got real old real fast."

"I think you're right on that. I'll call her and make an appointment to see her. I'll tell her what Greg told me, about his cancer, as well as your gift."

"Thanks, Mike. At least I'll feel that I've done something right, although I'm not so sure my brother would agree with me."

"Jess, Scott is the one who made his life what it is. You didn't make any of those decisions for him. Don't ever feel guilty for not lending him the money. It's quite evident what your father's intent was in this situation, and you saving Scott was not his intent."

"I know. It's just one more thing I have to deal with. Actually, this isn't the first time Scott has asked me for money. Matter-of-fact, I'd hate to count how many times he has."

"Well, Jess, I'd be willing to bet he'll never ask you for money again."

"Yeah, who knew there would be a silver lining in Dad's death? Not me."

"I'll call you after I meet with Rae Ann, and like I said at the beginning of this conversation, call me anytime."

"Thanks, Mike. I've gotta' go. Bully's standing next to the door with a frantic look in his eyes. Talk to you later."

CHAPTER TWELVE

After ending his call with Jessica, Mike picked up his phone and pressed in Rae Ann's telephone number, using the contact information Greg had given him.

A moment later the phone was answered by a woman and Mike said, "Hello, this is Sheriff Reynolds. I'd like to speak with Rae Ann Burns."

There was a pause, then the woman said, "This is Rae Ann."

"Mrs. Burns, I need to talk to you. Is there any chance you could meet with me about 1:00 today? I'd come to your home."

Again there was a pause, as if Rae Ann was trying to figure out why the Beaver County Sheriff would drive to her home to talk to her. "Yes, Sheriff, that would be fine. Can you tell me what this is about?" she asked.

"I'd rather tell you in person, but I want to assure that I'm not investigating you."

"Well, that's a relief. Do you have my address?"

"Yes, I'll see you at 1:00," Mike said as he ended the call.

*****

"Mrs. Burns?" Mike asked as an attractive woman in her 50's opened the door at the address he'd been given by Greg.

"Yes, that's me. You must be Sheriff Reynolds. Please, come in. Don't worry about Sadie," she said nodding towards a blond cocker spaniel who was sitting on a dog bed in the corner of the living room.

"Pretty dog. My wife and I are dog lovers. We have three dogs."

"Well, you're probably smart. Sadie is fifteen years old and the vet has told me she won't be with me much longer. I know I should probably get another dog because it would be easier for me if I had one when she goes, but I can't bring myself to do it. I'm afraid it would hurt her feelings. But you didn't come here to talk about Sadie," she said as she sat down in the chair next to where Mike was seated.

Mike took a deep breath and said, "No, Sadie isn't the reason I'm here. I understand you were in a relationship with Greg Tuttle. I also understand that you're aware he died in a boating accident the night before last."

Rae Ann's face crumpled. "I was hoping you were coming here to tell me that the report of his death was just some sick joke. Please tell me you're not really a sheriff and somebody is trying to play a joke on me, because if a sheriff tells me Greg is dead, that means it's real." Tears filled her eyes.

"I wish I could, Rae Ann. Here's my card, and unfortunately, it's not a joke. It's the truth. Here's what we know so far." For the next fifteen minutes he told her everything he knew about how Greg had died. The tears that had filled her eyes brimmed over and she silently cried during the entire conversation.

When Mike was finished, he sat back and became quiet, wanting to give her time to compose herself. After a few minutes she said, "Why did you come here to tell me this? How did you know where to find me?"

"My wife had a conversation yesterday at a dog kennel we use for our dogs with the daughter of a good friend of yours. Evidently you had visited her yesterday morning and were quite upset that you'd heard Greg had died. Evidently he'd also ended your relationship."

"Yes, that's true. He actually told me he was ending our relationship about a week ago. I kept thinking he'd call and say he'd made a mistake, but two days ago I realized he'd meant it when he said he didn't want to see me anymore."

"Do you know why he told you that?" Mike asked.

"I assumed it was because his wife had found out about us. He told me his marriage was dead, but he didn't want to go through another divorce."

"Part of that was true. He didn't want to go through the expense of another divorce, but he loved you very much. You see, I was his closest friend, and he named me as the trustee of his trust. We met a week or so ago and that's when he told me he had terminal cancer and the doctor had given him three months to live, at the most. That's also when he told me about you. The reason he broke off his relationship with you was so that you could go on with your life, instead of staying with a dying man."

"Oh my God! Oh no! Greg had incurable cancer? Why didn't he tell me? I loved him enough I gladly would have stayed with him to the end. I'd even served my husband with divorce papers. I loved Greg more than I thought was ever possible."

"If it's any consolation, and I'm sure it's not, he loved you just as much. He loved you so much he didn't want you to have to deal with the pain of losing him to cancer."

"But you told me he died from a boating accident. How could that happen? Greg was an experienced boater, and I know he and his wife went to that restaurant located on the waterfront of the bay probably five nights a week. He'd motored over there and back in his boat so many times he could have done it in his sleep. She did it, I know she did."

"What do you mean?"

"Somehow, his wife caused that accident. I don't know much about boats, but I'd bet everything I have that she's responsible for his death. She poisoned his drink or something. She didn't love him anymore, but she didn't want to leave him because of the money. Maybe he told her about us, and she was scared he'd leave her and she'd no longer have a rich husband. Although her boyfriend isn't all that rich, either."

"Her boyfriend? Do you know if she had a boyfriend, and if so, who is he?"

"Greg always suspected she was having an affair with her personal trainer at the fitness center. Think his name is Johnny Larson. Because Greg and I were having an affair, he never said anything to her about it. As a matter of fact, I think it made him feel less guilty."

"Well, that fits. Greg had told me he thought she was having an affair. I probably should look into this Johnny guy."

"I think you should. Look into it and see if Johnny and Susie were the ones behind Greg's death. What has the coroner said about the cause of death?"

"At this point, nothing. I called his office just before I came here, but there was a shooting out at a mall on the other side of the county. Unfortunately, three people were killed and the coroner has to do their autopsies immediately so the District Attorney can charge the shooter, but he needs to have the cause of death confirmed. I was told Greg's autopsy would probably be done early tomorrow."

"Would you let me know what he finds out? Greg may have had cancer, but other than that, I think he was healthy. In fact, when we first started seeing each other he told me his doctor said his body was twenty years younger than his age. Greg was glad to hear that, because his father had died from a heart attack at a relatively young age. Greg was very careful about what he ate." She sobbed and wiped her eyes, but tears continued to stream down her cheeks.

"Rae Ann, there's something else I need to tell you. It's a good thing, at least I think you'll consider it to be." Mike took a deep breath and said, "I don't know how much Greg told you about his children."

"Actually, quite a bit. I've never had children, so I asked him a lot of questions about them. He was very proud of his daughter and seemed to be quite close to her. I know they talked on the phone every couple of days and texted each other several times a day. And he loved her daughters, his grandchildren. He had nothing but good things to say about all of them. Even his son-in-law."

"Yes, Jessica is a very fine young woman, and I know he was very proud of her."

Rae Ann wiped her eyes again and said, "That's pretty much in direct contrast to how he felt about his son. He blamed himself for his son turning out to be a 'surface person.' At least those were the words Greg used to describe him. He told me all his son and daughter-in-law cared about was show, from their house to their car. Once he told me he'd probably never see the money he'd loaned his son and that his son wanted even more money from Greg, which he'd refused to give him."

"I'd say that's a fair assessment of how he felt about his son, and the terms of his trust reflects that," Mike said. "I don't feel comfortable going into the intricacies of the trust with you, because a trust document is private and confidential, however, Jessica stands to inherit quite a bit."

"From the way Greg talked on occasion, I guessed he was worth a lot of money, but not only did it not matter to me, we just never discussed numbers."

"Yes, Greg has a sizeable estate. I don't know if you're aware that he'd told Jessica about you, and she was very happy for him. She knew how much he loved you, and while he couldn't provide for you in his trust, Jessica is going to give you the sum of $100,000 from her share of the trust. She knows in the scheme of things it's not all that much, but at least you'll have something."

"Please thank her for me, Sheriff. That's extremely generous of her, but I don't need her money. I'm a financial consultant, and I have clients throughout the United States, so fortunately money is not a problem for me. What I appreciate more than anything is her knowing that her father cared for me. That's what will stay with me."

"I'll tell her what you said, but Greg had his moments of stubbornness, and I would have to say that Jessica definitely inherited that trait from him. Don't be surprised if a check from her arrives in your mail box in a couple of months. And a word of advice to you. The money is given freely, and I think it would hurt her feelings if you rejected it."

Rae Ann looked down at her hands for several long moments, then when she looked up at Mike, her eyes were once again filled with tears. "Sheriff, I know you didn't have to drive over here to see me. What you had to say could have been done by phone, but I want you to know how very much I appreciate your coming here to personally tell me about Greg."

"I'd like to say it was my pleasure, but that would be a lie. Delivering news of this type is never a pleasure. I wish it could have been good news," he said as he stood up and prepared to leave.

"So do I, Sheriff, so do I. But do me one favor. Get to the bottom of Greg's death. He didn't fall overboard accidentally. Please investigate this thoroughly and find out who's responsible for his death. And take a long, long, look at Susie. Don't the cop shows on TV say you always look at who has the most to gain? Well, she did."

"In fact, in the end she didn't," he said enigmatically as he opened the door and started to walk out. "Greg took care of that."

CHAPTER THIRTEEN

Okay, Mike thought, *the restaurant often lets some of its servers take a break between the lunch and dinner services, so I might as well go to Jack's Marine Repair now and then stop by the restaurant. I'd like to see how much damage Greg's inflatable did to the other boat. Josh told me the owner was going to take it there as soon as he could.*

He drove down to the bay and took the road that hugged it to Jack's, which was at the far end of the bay. Jack's was the only boat repair in Cedar Bay, and it always seemed to do a very good business. He parked his car in the last available empty spot in the lot, glad the parking fairy was with him. There were several tourist shops near Jack's and in the summertime, parking was always at a premium.

When he opened the door at Jack's Marine Repair, he heard a voice say, "Well, Sheriff, kind of figured you might come calling today. Bet you want to see the boat that Tuttle's inflatable did a number on."

Mike blinked for a moment or two, the sun having hit him square in the eyes when he'd opened the door. He looked behind the desk and saw Jack West, the owner of the boat repair.

"Good to see you, Jack, and yes, that's why I'm here."

"Figured that, since I can't get you to buy a boat, even if you do live on the bay and have a dock."

"I know, but you have to admit since we live on the cliff above the bay, that walking down one hundred and sixty steps to get to the dock and the boat, and then back up again, isn't my idea of a good time. Certainly not at my age. Plus, as we've talked about before, boats are nothing more than an endless money drain."

"All true," the grizzled large man said, his skin the color of mahogany from being outdoors all day, "but you left out a very important component."

"What's that?" Mike asked.

"I'd be the recipient of the endless money drain. It's not like you wouldn't know where your money was going."

"That's true, but from what I've seen, you don't need any more business. You're probably the wealthiest man in Cedar Bay."

"Wouldn't go that far," Jack said with a grin, "but those boats sure do help pay the medical school costs for my son and the law school costs for my daughter. As soon as they're finished with their education, I'm outta' here. Planning on going to Mexico and let them support me for a change. Live the high life. Find a senorita, eat mangos, drink tequila, and get a tan."

"First of all, if you get any darker, Doc Burkham is going to be asking you to come into his office to check you over for skin problems, secondly, you'd be bored in a matter of days."

"Yeah, you're probably right. Okay, let me show you the bad boy that was the recipient of the crash. Don't know what the owner's insurance is, but it's going to be seriously expensive just to replace the teak on the damaged boat. Follow me. The boat's so big I had to put it at the far end of my dock."

They walked past a number of boats tied up to the dock with Jack's employees working on them. At the far end of the dock Mike saw the boat Greg's inflatable had hit. It was a beauty, an old boat with a lot of teak and brass.

"Jack, how much is it going to take to fix it?"

"I think about $65,000. Teak is really expensive and as you can see, there's a major league hole in the rear transom area. The teak swim step on the rear of the boat was demolished by the force of the impact."

"That's a shame," Mike said. "It really is a beauty. I'm surprised Susie didn't get hurt when the boat hit. After all, she was sitting in the front of the dinghy. I asked her why she didn't get up and pull the throttle back after Greg fell in the water, and she told me Greg had always told her to never stand up in the boat when it was underway. He told her he was seaworthy enough that he could steer the boat when he was standing up, but she was never to stand in it."

Mike looked over at Jack who had a strange expression on his face.

"Jack, what are you thinking?"

"I'd like to know what you're smoking, to begin with, Sheriff. First of all, there is no way Susie was sitting where she told you she was. If she had been, with as much force as that inflatable hit this boat, she would have been killed outright from the force of the impact. Think about it, Mike. No way."

"I hadn't thought about it, but after seeing the extent of the damage to the boat, I'd probably have to agree with you."

"Secondly, Mike. She's nuts. She's driven that inflatable in here more times than I can count, and each time she was standing up. I don't know what kind of a game she's playing, but something is very wrong with that scenario."

"Oh boy. You certainly have given me plenty of food for thought. Speaking of which, Jack, you evidently know the Tuttles. Have any thoughts on what went down with him falling overboard?"

Jack was quiet for several moments and appeared to be in deep thought, then he said, "I always considered Greg Tuttle to be one of the finest men I've ever known. He always treated me like an equal, unlike a lot of rich men who bring their boats in here. His wife is another story. I always had the feeling she was just in the marriage for the money. I never saw any true affection between them. If anything, she seemed to belittle him constantly.

"If theirs was some kind of a role model marriage, I don't want any part of it. As you know, my wife died several years ago, and I've thought of remarrying from time to time, but every time the Tuttles came in here, it reinforced why I haven't remarried. Don't need that kind of a woman in my life."

"Quite frankly, I think Greg agreed with you. Thanks, Jack. I don't know what I'll do with what you've told me, but I've found when a number of people tell me things, a pattern starts to develop, and in this case, what started out looking like a simple case of a man falling overboard is now taking on another dimension. Maybe several dimensions."

"Need anything more from me, Sheriff? If not, think I better get back to my work. This time of year we're working from sunup to sundown. Only saving grace is that it stays light pretty late in the day here in Oregon. Makes up for those short winter days. Let me know if I can help," Jack said as he hurried back towards his shop.

I wonder if Susie could have been involved in Greg's death, and if so, how? Rae Ann certainly thought she had something to do with it. This is really getting convoluted. Maybe I'll find out something at the restaurant, Mike thought as he walked back to his car.

CHAPTER FOURTEEN

By the time Kelly got to Kelly's Koffee Shop, it was two hours later than her usual opening time of 6:00 a.m. The place was packed with breakfast diners, people picking up some sweet rolls and coffee to take to work with them, and people meeting friends before their day started.

She waved at Roxie who was busy serving orders and walked back to the kitchen to check in with Charlie, her long-time cook. "Morning, Charlie. How's everything going?"

"No problems, Kelly. Heard you were back. Sorry that your vacation didn't work out, but it always feels better when you're here. We were really busy yesterday, and from the looks of it, today's going to be the same."

"Thanks for making it run smoothly, Charlie," Kelly said as she walked back to the storeroom where the aprons were kept. She put hers on and walked out to the dining area.

"Roxie, I'll take care of the cash register and seating people. You just do what you do best, charm the customers by taking their orders."

"Will do, boss. Glad you're back. Want me to tell Poppy that we won't need her this week since you're back?"

"No, I'm sure she was counting on the money, plus having her help by serving and busing the orders will give you a little rest. You do so much as it is, I'm glad she can take on some of what you do."

"Okay, I'll go tell her. She didn't say anything when I told her about your vacation that didn't happen, but I could sense she wondered if she'd be able to work this week. I know you don't need to do this, but both of us will benefit. Thanks from both of us," she said as she walked towards Poppy.

The coffee shop stayed busy all morning with a steady stream of customers coming and going, most of them known to Kelly. Kelly was ringing up a customer when Doc Burkham walked in. Kelly could count on one hand the number of times he'd missed showing up for lunch since he'd moved to Cedar Bay several years earlier, married the local psychologist, and taken over Doctor Amherst's practice.

"Good to see you, Kelly, but sorry your vacation didn't work out."

"Thanks, Doc. I'm sorry too, but under the circumstances we didn't have a choice. Mike and Greg go back a long way, and there was no way Mike felt he could go to Hawaii. Plus, not only did Greg name him as the trustee of his trust, Greg's daughter, Jessica, is Mike's goddaughter."

"Yeah, I knew Greg was his trustee. Between you and me, Kelly, I think this may have been a blessing in disguise."

"Doc, I'm surprised to hear that from you. What do you mean?"

"Kelly, Greg had a mean kind of cancer and the last days of his life were not going to be pleasant. Something like that tears apart a family, and from what Greg had told me, which I'm sure is no secret to you, that family already had some major problems. In addition to the physical pain he'd be in, I'm sure there would be emotional pain as well. I've been at this long enough to know that God works in mysterious ways."

"I hadn't thought about it like that, but you're probably right. Doc," Kelly said, looking down the aisle, "it looks like Roxie saved your favorite booth for you. Better hurry before somebody tries to take it away from you. And by the way, the salmon with a tomato béarnaise sauce is fabulous. A friend of Charlie's went up to British Columbia and brought back more salmon than his family could eat, so we bought what we could from him."

"Thanks for the tip, Kelly. I'll let Roxie know that's what I want," he said as he walked towards his booth.

CHAPTER FIFTEEN

"Hi, Kelly, think you got room in here for me?" a familiar voice said a few minutes later.

She turned around and saw Pete, Roxie's brother. Pete had been a huge help to Kelly when Mike had a bad case of the flu and solving a murder that occurred at a truck stop outside of Cedar Bay had pretty much fallen on her shoulders. Several of the truckers had worked for Pete, and she and Pete had developed a mutually respected friendship.

"Are you kidding, Pete? Can you imagine what Roxie would do to me if I didn't find a place for her brother? As important as your sister is to this establishment, if something happened to her, I might as well close the doors. It's my personal opinion, pretty much based on fact, that most of the customers who come in here on any given day do so because of Roxie's warmth and her great smile. The first time they meet her, they know they have a friend for life."

"Yeah, trust me, it wasn't easy being in her shadow when we were growing up. I tend to appraise people for a while before I want to let them into my world. Obviously, that way of making friends is quite the opposite of hers, so guess who had more friends growing up? Bingo, you're right," he said with a laugh as he formed a gun out of his fingers and pointed it at Kelly.

Kelly laughed as well. "Follow me, Pete. I can see a bunch more people coming in, and I want to make sure you have a booth."

He sat down at the indicated booth and Kelly handed him a menu. "I'm only telling my favorite people this, Pete, but you better order the salmon. It's a special today, and there is a very limited supply. With this lunch crowd, I expect it won't be available for very much longer. I see Roxie coming over, so make sure she takes your order to Charlie right away. Talk to you later."

She started to walk away, but Pete put a hand on her arm. "Kelly, I didn't come here just for lunch. When you get a moment, I need to talk to you."

She started to make a smart comeback, then looked down at his serious expression and said, "Pete is everything alright?"

"With me, yes, but I saw something the night Greg Tuttle died that I think your husband needs to know about. I've never met your husband, so I thought I'd see if maybe you'd be the messenger. I heard he was very close to Tuttle, and I'm sure he's probably doing some grieving of his own."

"He is, but he's also the trustee of Greg's trust, so that's taking precedence right now. Plus, Greg died in a boating accident in a bay that's in Mike's jurisdiction. He also has to try and determine how Greg fell out of the boat. You know, due diligence and all of that."

"Yes, I understand. I'll wait here until you have a minute."

*****

Forty-five minutes later, the crowd thinned out in the coffee shop, and Kelly walked back to the booth where Pete was sitting.

"I can see from your clean plate that the salmon was a hit," Kelly said, as she sat down across from him.

"You think?" he asked jokingly as he gestured towards his plate.

"Good, I'm glad you liked it. It's pretty rare we get fresh caught salmon to serve, and there's no comparison between it and the salmon you buy at the store. All you have to do is look at the difference in color and that's before you even compare the tastes.

"As a food lover and someone who really wants to make eating here a good experience for my customers, I can't, in good conscience, serve that stuff you get at the store. That's the reason why you won't see salmon on the menu here. Now, what did you want to talk to me about?"

"Kelly, this may be nothing or it may be something, but either way, I feel your husband needs to know about it."

"That certainly whets my curiosity."

"Let me start out by asking what the coroner has determined was the cause of Greg's death. Do you know?"

"No, and the reason being that the coroner had to delay the autopsy for a day because of a shooting in a mall on the far side of the county. Mike expects to get it sometime today. Why are you asking?"

Pete ran one of his hands over his face and then looked across the table at Kelly. "I saw something the night Greg died that may have a bearing on the cause of his death."

"Okay, Pete, you have my full attention. I'll be right back. I want to tell Roxie to take over for me." She slipped out of the booth and walked over to where Roxie was standing. Pete could see her talking earnestly to his sister and then he saw Roxie nod her head. Kelly walked back to the booth and sat down across from him."

"I'm all ears, Pete."

"I don't know if what I'm about to tell you is relevant to Greg's death, but I think it probably is. I haven't slept well the last two nights thinking about it, wondering if what I saw was the reason he fell overboard. He took a deep breath and then a long drink of water.

"Sometimes after dinner when the kids have gone to bed and my wife is watching television, I like to take a little inflatable I keep at the Cedar Bay dock out on the bay. You know, kind of to clear my head from business. I know if I stay in my office at home, which I usually do after dinner, I'll just get immersed in work, go to bed, wake up in the morning, and go back to work all over again."

"Yes, I like to have a little time away from the coffee shop for the same reason, not that I'm unhappy with what I'm doing or anything like that, but a change of pace from time to time seems to help."

"Exactly. Well, night before last I got to the dock about 8:00, took my boat out on the bay to the place where I usually go. I turned the engine off, threw out the anchor, and just sat there nice and still. It was quiet and dark, a moonless night. I like to look at the lights on the boats and the ones on shore. May sound crazy, but it relaxes me."

"I understand."

"I'd been sitting there for maybe fifteen minutes, when a kayak glided in front of me. I don't have any running lights on my inflatable, and I'd turned off the engine and the light I use on the bow of the boat when I'm under way. I don't think the kayak saw me. As I said earlier, it was a moonless night."

"Yes, I know. We were at the Portland airport waiting for our flight to Hawaii. I remember thinking how dark it was outside and said something to my son about how it was a good thing planes had radar and lights, because there is no way anyone could see to fly on a completely moonless night."

"Anyway, Kelly, this kayak stopped not too far from me with it's bow pointing towards The Waterfront Restaurant. We were both about two-thirds of the distance between the restaurant and the houses on the other side of the bay, so we had a good view of the restaurant.

"A couple came out of the restaurant and got in an inflatable boat. I couldn't see them very well, and I have no idea where they were sitting in their boat or who was driving. They turned on the boat's running lights and headed for the houses behind us."

"That would be the houses where the Tuttles lived, right?" Kelly asked.

"Yes. The kayak was slightly ahead of me and as the inflatable came closer, I could see that a man and a woman were standing up in the inflatable, the man I now know to have been Greg Tuttle. When the boat was directly in front of us, say thirty feet away, the person in the kayak who appeared to be a man raised his arm and it looked like he fired a gun at the man in the boat."

"You're kidding. Do you know who that person was?"

"Not by name," Pete said. "One time I mentioned something about seeing a kayaker on the water often at night and someone at the dock said that it was a guy who was a personal trainer at the fitness center. The person said the trainer did kayaking to stay in shape, but could only do it at night because he worked in the fitness center during the day."

"Okay, that gives us an idea of who it was. What happened after you saw him fire the gun, if that's what it was?"

"That's what's been keeping me up at night, Kelly. I never heard anything, like a gunshot, but the man standing in the boat, Greg Tuttle, fell overboard. His boat took off and sped forward, then it began turning in high speed circles. It eventually straightened out and crashed into a large boat that was docked at one of the houses."

"Did you go over to where Greg had fallen in the water?"

"No, several other people with larger boats were on the water and able to quickly respond. The woman in the inflatable cried out for help, and within minutes, the place was a madhouse. I knew immediately that my boat was too small to help. I heard bullhorns from a police helicopter overhead as well as people shouting from the shore. There were multiple police and sheriff's sirens. They were all far better equipped to deal with what was happening than I was."

"Did you notice what happened to the person in the kayak?"

"No. Obviously my attention was riveted to the scene unfolding in front of me. When I thought to look around for the kayak, it was gone. I motored back to the dock to tie my boat up and when I was there, I looked over to where the kayak was usually tied up. It wasn't there. I don't know what happened to it."

"What did you do then, Pete?"

"I hung around the dock for a while with a lot of other people. We could see that the Coast Guard had pulled Greg out of the water, but from where we were standing, it looked like he was dead. I felt sick to my stomach and went home.

"When I got there, I turned on the news. The local station had interrupted their show with the news of a drowning in Cedar Bay. The name was not revealed until the next of kin had been notified. I didn't know until the next morning that it was Greg Tuttle."

Kelly took a long breath and then said, "You mentioned a gun, Pete, but when Mike spoke to his deputy on the way home from the Portland airport, he specifically asked him if there were any signs of foul play. The deputy told him that there weren't. Surely if a gunshot was strong enough to cause someone to fall overboard, there would be some sign of a bullet entry on the body, to say nothing of blood."

"I thought the same thing, and I've come up with an alternative off-the-wall answer. And Kelly, please understand I know next to nothing about guns or law enforcement, but I recently happened to be reading a magazine in my dentist's office. He's a big supporter of the NRA, and he had some of their magazines on a coffee table in the reception area. I picked one up and read about a new liquid stun gun that had a longer range than other stun guns or tasers."

"So you think the kayak guy could have used a stun gun?"

"I have no clue, however, let me tell you something else I read about that type of gun. It uses liquid and you can fire it a number of successive times very quickly, as opposed to other types of stun guns. However, because you need to cart the conductive liquid around, they can be quite cumbersome. It went on to say that portable models typically include a water tank backpack."

"I think I know where this is going, Pete. The man in the kayak had something bulky on his back, but you couldn't identify it."

"Yes, that's it exactly. When he passed in front of me, I was looking at his profile, and he definitely had something bulky on his back. It was not the normal profile of a man."

"And if he used some kind of a stun gun, there wouldn't be any signs of foul play," Kelly said, nodding her head.

"I'm assuming that's true, but intellectually I'd think there would be some internal signs, even if there were no outward signs. I don't know much about these things, but I think that type of gun works on or shocks the human nervous system. I'm wondering if it will show up in the autopsy."

"Good question. What I'm thinking is that if someone used a stun gun on Greg and it caused him to fall in the water, he might have had too much to drink at the restaurant and his reflexes were slowed down because of his alcohol consumption.

"I know Greg was a strong swimmer and often swam in the bay, so he should easily have been able to get back to the boat, but between being stunned and maybe having consumed too much alcohol, he couldn't. You said the boat Greg was in kept going and then started turning in circles. Was it trying to find him?"

"I don't think so. It looked like it was too far away from Greg when it went around in circles. I gathered it was because Greg had fallen overboard and was no longer driving it."

"Pete, I think I read something once about a person's family suing the police because the person had been tased by the police. The person suffered a fatal heart attack which they attributed to being tased."

"I think I've heard the same thing, but I don't know if it it's been proven or if it was just a lawsuit. Just because someone sues for something doesn't mean it's true."

"No, I agree, but here's where I was going with that. If Greg was tased, maybe it caused him to have a heart attack and fall overboard. Maybe he died from a heart attack, instead of by drowning. I guess we'll know when we get the coroner's report."

"Kelly, I really need to get back to work. Would you do me a favor and call me when Mike finds out from the coroner the cause of Greg's death? Having been there and seeing what I did, I admit I'm curious. And if the tasing led to Greg's death, could the guy in the kayak be arrested for murder, even if the official cause of death is listed as drowning?"

"I don't know the answer to that question, but think about it. If a guy is standing on a steel construction beam and someone pushes him off of it and he falls forty stories to his death, wouldn't the guy who pushed him off be arrested for murder? My gut reaction is yes, but then again, I'm not in law enforcement."

"You may not be in law enforcement, but I think a lot of Mike's involvement in it has rubbed off on you. Don't downplay what you know."

"Thanks, Pete. I'll call you when Mike tells me about the results of the autopsy. I'll tell Mike what you told me, and who knows? You may have solved a murder case before the investigation even gets started."

"To tell you the truth, Kelly, I wish I'd stayed home that night. There are a couple of visuals I'm having trouble with, and I think I'll probably be haunted by them for some time."

"Yes, I can see where you would be," Kelly said as he handed her his check for his meal and cash to cover it. "Talk to you later."

CHAPTER SIXTEEN

Mike hadn't really thought of Greg's death as being anything but an unfortunate accident, but his conversations with Rae Ann and Jack were making him think otherwise. And on the surface, Rae Ann was right. Susie would be the most logical suspect, but Scott would also have to be high up there on the list.

As he was driving to The Waterfront Restaurant, several thoughts about Greg's death occurred to him.

I suppose, even though it's a longshot, that maybe Susie and her boyfriend thought that if Greg was dead, and she inherited 1/3 of his estate, they could blissfully walk off into the sunset with a couple of million dollars.

If I was conducting a regular investigation case, I'd look at Susie, Scott, and Susie's boyfriend. I think I better take off my hat as trustee and wear my sheriff's hat until I find out a few things.

Oh, and something else. I remember when we were at the house yesterday Susie's sister said something about there was no way Susie was going to live with her. Maybe Susie told her about the cancer and Kendra did something to insure that wouldn't happen. Actually, when I think about it, there are quite a few suspects.

Josh was at the bay when the Coast Guard recovered Greg's body. I specifically asked him if there were any signs of foul play, and he said no. That would include bullet holes, knife wounds, or anything else, which means if someone did do something to him, it would have affected him internally.

A short time later, Mike pulled into the parking lot of The Waterfront Restaurant, the restaurant where Susie and Greg had eaten the night he died. He wanted to talk with the owner, Sam, and whoever had served Greg that night. He didn't know exactly what he was looking for, but he wanted to cover everything that could possibly be related to Greg's death.

After he parked his car and entered the restaurant, he approached the hostess stand. "Hi, Sheriff, how can I help you? Table for one?" the hostess asked.

"No, thanks. I was wondering if Sam or Mitzi is here."

"Sam's out of town for a couple of days, but Mitzi's here. Let me get her for you."

A few minutes later, Mitzi walked out of the kitchen and said, "Hey, Sheriff. It's good to see you. Sure was sorry to hear about Greg. He was without a doubt our best customer and everybody here loved him. He's going to sincerely be missed, and not just for his tips, which were always quite generous."

"Actually, Mitzi, that's why I'm here. I was wondering if you were his server that night."

"No, I had to take the day off. My sister's pregnant and she was having some problems. My brother-in-law had to make a run, he's a truck driver, and he didn't want her to be alone, so he asked me if I could come and stay with her. I left the morning Greg died and returned this morning."

"Who took your shift?"

"A waitress named Lydia. She's here now, if you'd like to talk to her. It's pretty slow right now, actually almost non-existent, so I'm sure she has the time."

"Yes, I would like to talk to her. Tell Lydia I'll meet her on the bench in front of the restaurant. It's a little more private out there."

"Will do," she said as she turned around and went back into the kitchen.

Mike stepped outside and sat down on the bench, looking at the bay. He thought how peaceful it looked, not like a place that could take a man's life. A moment later the door opened and a young woman with short black hair walked out of the restaurant.

"You must be the sheriff Mitzi told me about. Would I be right?" she asked.

"Yes. I'm Sheriff Reynolds, Lydia. Please sit down. I'd like to ask you a few questions, if you don't mind."

"Not at all. I'm sorry about your friend, Mr. Tuttle. He was a nice man."

"Thank you. I'm really not sure where to go with this, so why don't you tell me what you remember about that night, if you would," Mike said.

"Sure, but you have to keep in mind that I'm pretty new here. As a matter of fact, that was the first time I'd served Mr. and Mrs. Tuttle."

"What was your impression of them?"

"He seemed very nice. He ordered a Scotch on the rocks, and she had a glass of white wine. He told me they'd order in a little while. He motioned for me to get them another round of drinks after a few minutes. When I took it to them, he said that would be the last round of drinks. His wife laughed and said something like, 'Don't be silly. Every day is a plus for us, so we're celebrating your life.' She told me to bring them a new round each time she motioned to me."

"Isn't that a little odd?" Mike asked.

"I sure thought so, but like I said, I'm pretty new here and I thought maybe that was just how the Tuttles did dinner."

"Did he say anything after she'd said that to you?"

"Yes. I can't give you the exact words, but it was something like 'Are you trying to get me drunk?' I thought it was kind of strange when she answered with, and I remember these words exactly. She said 'At this point, does it really matter?' He laughed and said he guessed not. Strange, huh?"

"Yeah," Mike said.

"Did they order dinner?"

"Yes. He had a chicken breast and some vegetables. She had a steak with a baked potato, but neither one of them finished their dinner. When the plates had been cleared, she asked for a brandy for each of them. He really didn't want it, but she convinced him they'd just have one and then head for home."

That's funny, Mike thought. *In all the years I've known Greg, I've never seen him drink brandy.*

"Lydia, what was your overall impression of Mr. and Mrs. Tuttle that night?"

She was quiet for a moment and then said, "We're not really supposed to talk about our customers, but since he's dead I guess it doesn't matter. Quite honestly, I thought she was really pushing the drinks on him. I don't think he wanted them, and overall, they probably had about seven rounds plus the brandy. That's a lot of alcohol.

"As a matter of fact, when I heard he'd fallen overboard and drowned, I wasn't that surprised. He was a big man, but even so, I'd bet his blood alcohol was way above the legal limit. I even wondered if she wanted him to fall overboard and that's why she pushed the drinks."

"Why would you think that?" Mike asked.

"Well, I'm probably talking out of school, but my sister works at the fitness center where Mrs. Tuttle goes. It's pretty common knowledge that she and Johnny, one of the trainers, are having an affair. The thought went through my mind that if Mr. Tuttle died and his wife inherited all his money, she and Johnny could really live in style."

She put her hand over her mouth and said, "I'm sorry. That was a horrible thing for me to say. Please forget I ever said it." She stood up. "I've really said more than I should, and I have to get back to work. It was nice meeting you, Sheriff." She opened the door to the restaurant and walked back inside.

Swell, Mike thought. *First, Rae Ann thinks Susie was responsible and now Lydia certainly hinted at it. So much for Greg just falling overboard. This is getting to be a lot more complicated than I thought it would be.*

Lost in thought, he didn't hear the restaurant door open. "Sheriff, do you have a minute?" Mitzi asked.

"Of course, Mitzi. Have a seat. What can I do for you?"

She sat down next to him and then began to softly cry. "Mitzi, what's wrong? Is it something about your sister and the baby?" he asked.

"No. I just need to tell you this. I feel so bad about Mr. Tuttle. Sheriff, I don't think his death was an accident."

That's just great, Mike thought. *Here's another person who's going to tell me why they think there was more to Greg's death than accidentally falling overboard.*

"Why do you think that?" Mike asked her.

"Because I did something horrible. No, I had nothing to do with his death, but I could have. No, I don't mean that either. Here's what happened."

"I'm listening, Mitzi."

"About a week ago I received a call from Susie's sister, Kendra. I'd met her a couple of times when she was visiting Greg and Susie and they'd come here for dinner. We talked for a few minutes about this and that. A few months earlier when she'd been here, I'd mentioned that my daughter was in her senior year in high school, and I hoped she'd be able to get a scholarship to college."

"Mitzi, I think every parent wishes their child would get a scholarship."

"Yes. Well, she remembered and asked if my daughter had gotten a scholarship. I told her so far she hadn't, but we were still waiting to hear from a couple of colleges. She told me she had a job for me that would pay $25,000 and that would sure help with college expenses."

"Yes, I'm sure it would. What was the job?" Mike asked.

"She said she'd pay me that amount if I'd put something in Greg's last drink of the night. She actually mentioned the night she wanted it done. It was the night he died."

"What did you tell her?" Mike asked.

"I told her I needed to think about it, and that I'd call her back."

"And did you?"

"Yes. I tossed and turned all night. I really wanted that money since things are pretty tight in my household, and there is no way I'm going to be able to scrape the money together to send my daughter to the college she wants to attend. That's why I'm so desperate for her to get a scholarship. But the next morning, I knew I could never do something like that and live with myself, no matter how badly I needed the money."

"So you called her and said no?" Mike asked.

"I called her after I'd had a cup of coffee, but I got her answerphone. I left a message that I couldn't do something like that, and that was the end of it. She never called me again. Once I made the call a huge feeling of relief swept over me. I knew I'd done the right thing. It was the only thing I could do and live with myself."

Mike reached over and patted her shoulder. "Yes, Mitzi, you did do the right thing, but now I'm beginning to wonder if someone else didn't. A thought just occurred to me. Is there any way Susie's sister could have known that Lydia had taken your shift?"

"No, not unless she called the restaurant that day and even then, from the way things go here at the restaurant, when someone is filling in for someone else, in other words taking over their shift, the decision is always made at the last minute based on the number of reservations."

"That's probably the only way a restaurant can handle that. So no one came in to sub for you?" Mike asked.

"No, the existing wait staff would just make the number of tables they served larger. Lydia expanded my table into the ones she'd already be serving that night. If you're thinking she had something to do with Greg's death, that's a dead end. There is no way anyone could have known she'd be serving the Tuttles until the last minute, far too late to get any plan in place."

"I see," Mike said. "From other people I've talked to, I'm getting a sense that there may be a lot more to Greg's death than drowning by falling overboard. And even though it seems a couple of people wanted him dead, that still doesn't mean his death wasn't caused by simply falling overboard and drowning.

"He may have even lost his balance from too much alcohol and fallen overboard, but I'm sure that will come out in the autopsy, which I should have tomorrow morning."

"Sheriff, I wish I could be of some help to you. I know Mr. Tuttle was a good friend of yours, and this has to be very difficult for you not only personally, but also professionally."

"Thanks, Mitzi. And yes, this may be the hardest case I've ever had to deal with. If you think of anything else or hear anything you think I should know about, please call me. And good luck with your daughter's scholarship. We could all use a little good news about now."

He stood up to leave and then said, "One last thing, Mitzi. You served Greg and Susie a number of times. You know they always drove their inflatable over here from their house across the bay. Do you know who usually drove it?"

"Oh sure, everyone knows that. It was kind of a running joke around here. Greg always drove it here to the restaurant and his wife always drove it home. The joke was that if they ever got a ticket for drunk driving, she'd be the one to get it, not him."

"Did they usually drink that much?"

"Not always, but often enough that it spawned the running joke."

"Thanks," Mike said as he headed towards his car.

CHAPTER SEVENTEEN

When Mike got in his car, he noticed that the restaurant parking lot was beginning to fill up. It was probably the best restaurant in Cedar Bay and certainly had the best view. *Sort of strange*, he thought, *that it could be the location where a plot to commit murder got started.*

I'm on overload right now and I need some time to think about what I've found out today, he thought. *Seeing Kelly and the dogs along with a good dinner will probably do wonders for my attitude and frame of mind.*

A few minutes later he pulled in his driveway, hit the button for the garage door opener, drove in, and got out of his car. Mike could hear the sound of yips coming from the other side of the door that led to the house. He was sure the dogs were there, waiting for him to pet them.

He opened the door and there they were. He did his evening ritual of telling them what good dogs they were, petted them, and then went into the kitchen. He walked over to Kelly who was standing at the kitchen counter and kissed her on the back of the neck.

"Hi, love," she said. "I'm just finishing up some prep work for dinner. Why don't you go in the great room and get comfortable? I'll meet you there in a couple of minutes, and we can share a little wine while we compare our days."

A few minutes later she walked into the great room with two glasses of wine. Mike was rubbing his eyes and looked tired. "Bad day, huh?" she asked as she handed him his glass and sat down.

"Yeah, a day when I got more questions than I did answers."

"Hate to tell you this, but I'm probably going to add to it. Why don't you start, and we're in absolutely no hurry. Take your time. If you'd rather go in and take a nap, we can do it later."

"No, Kelly, I like to bounce things off of you. Let me start with Rae Ann."

"What did you think of her?"

"I liked her. As a matter of fact, I wish Greg had met her before he met Susie. She's a class act."

"From that I'm inferring that you don't think Susie is."

"Not from what I heard today. She was never my favorite, but now I'm pretty sure she's a liar. Anyway, here's what Rae Ann told me." He related his conversation with Rae Ann and finished up with, "My heart really goes out to her. Kind of a case of unrequited love on both of their parts."

"How did she take Jessica's gracious gift to her?"

"In a class manner. She thanked me for it, but said she didn't need it. Evidently she has a very good job and the man she's divorcing is quite wealthy, so she told me that money was no object."

"That's something you don't hear all that often," Kelly said.

"No, and it was refreshing."

"But knowing you and knowing Jessica's wishes, you insisted, right?"

"You know me too well," Mike answered. "When I left, I felt really sorry for both her and for Greg. I wish they'd had time to enjoy their relationship a little longer. Doesn't seem fair."

"I agree, but I think I read somewhere that life isn't fair. I'd have to agree with that statement. So, she's pretty much out of the picture now other than giving her a check when the money from the trust is distributed."

"Yes. I'm sorry you didn't get to meet her, because I think you really would have liked her."

"Who knows? Maybe I will. What interests me is that from what you just told me, she was very adamant that Susie had something to do with Greg's death."

"Very, very adamant, and I have to say, based on what I found out at Jack's, there may be some truth to it, although I can't make it all fit with what I now know."

"What did you find out at Jack's and how badly damaged was the other boat?"

"The boat was really torn up and Jack definitely does not like Susie. Here's what he had to say about both."

When he was finished, Kelly said, "Interesting that she apparently lied about where she was sitting in the boat. Why do you think she did that?"

"I have no idea. I'd think maybe Jack had it in for her for some reason, like maybe she'd been rude to him, or tried to stiff him on some job, or whatever. But here's the thing, Mitzi at the restaurant pretty much confirmed that Susie always drove the boat home from the restaurant."

"Was she the one who served them the night he died?"

"No, however, I was able to talk to the server who did. Here's what she said." Mike told Kelly about his conversation with Lydia.

"Wow, that's a lot of alcohol. I'll be curious to see what his blood alcohol level was when you get the results of the autopsy."

"So will I, but I'm sure it was over the legal limit. Mitzi confirmed that he and Susie often drank a lot when they were at the restaurant, but does it play into his death? That's what's becoming crucial."

"At this point we don't know, but Mike, it sure sounds like Susie was pushing the drinks the night he died."

"That was Lydia's take on it as well. There's something more that Mitzi told me about Susie's sister, Kendra. Evidently she wanted to pay Mitzi a lot of money to slip something into Greg's drink."

"You're kidding. Why would she be involved in his death, and what did Mitzi say?"

"Even though Mitzi really could have used the money for her daughter's college education, she turned it down. She wasn't even at the restaurant the night Greg died. She had to go to her sister's. I haven't checked her alibi out, but I rather doubt that I need to at this point."

"Could her sister have paid the server who took care of Susie and Greg the night he died to do something?"

"Not according to Mitzi. I explored that possibility with her and the way the restaurant determines how a server takes a table when they have to cover for each other is pretty random. I don't think there's any way Susie's sister could have found out in time to do anything, considering the server herself didn't even know until minutes before that she was going to be assigned that table. No, that's not a possibility."

"Okay, but back to my other question. Why would Susie's sister do something like that?"

"I have no idea. I met her when I went to Susie's house yesterday and her sister made some comment about Susie not living with her. In all honesty, I didn't pay much attention to it. She said it after Lem had explained the terms of the trust. Maybe she did it because Susie had told her what Greg planned to do with his trust and she was afraid Susie would move in with her because she wouldn't have enough money to live on her own."

"That seems a bit of a stretch, but then again, we've seen some weird reasons why people do things. Think about it while I get us another glass of wine. What I have to tell you will probably confuse you even more, if that's possible."

CHAPTER EIGHTEEN

"Seriously, Kelly, what you're going to tell me is going to confuse me even more?" he asked as she walked back in the room and handed him his wine.

"Yes, as you know, I went to the coffee shop this morning. Everything was fine, but I knew it would be with Roxie handling it. Doc came in as usual and had a take on Greg's death that I hadn't considered. He told me that given the kind of cancer Greg had, his falling overboard may have been a blessing, because that kind of cancer is usually very painful."

"I'd never considered that either. I've been operating on the thought that Greg's death was a tragedy, but maybe not."

"Before I tell you about my meeting with Pete, let me ask you this. You don't think that Susie was trying to commit some type of mercy killing, do you? You know, like make Greg's balance be off from all the alcohol, then drive the boat in a way, that in his state, affected his balance, and he falls overboard and drowns. She might think it was better to have him die from drowning rather than suffer a painful death from cancer."

"Even after all we've seen of human nature, you still like to believe in people, don't you, and that's a wonderful trait. However, while I think it's a nice thought, sweetheart, I don't think Susie is the type of person who is capable of doing an act of mercy for someone. Plus, I've heard from several people, including Greg himself, that the marriage was over. I'm gathering there was no love lost between either of them.

"Jack even said he thought she treated Greg horribly. I'm becoming pretty convinced that the only thing Susie thinks about is Susie. So, tell me Kelly, what is going to confuse me?"

"Do you remember me talking about Pete, Roxie's brother, when I was helping you solve the murder that occurred at the truck stop, and what a help he was to me?"

"Yes, and from what I remember you liked him a lot."

"That's true. He came into the coffee shop today, because although he thought he should tell you what he'd seen, he'd never met you, so he felt that I would be a good messenger."

"I'm all ears. What's the message?"

She told him what Pete had seen and what Pete had learned about a liquid stun gun, as well as his thoughts on Greg's drowning. When she was finished, Mike was quiet for several minutes, deep in thought.

"Well, what do you think?" Kelly finally asked.

"You were right. I'm even more confused now. I have Susie's sister who apparently wanted to kill Greg by having a server put something in his drink. I have Susie who lied to me about where she was sitting in the boat. I have a kayaker who very well may have shot Greg with a liquid stun gun, and who apparently is the man who is having an affair with Susie.

"The motives are bothering me. The kayaker's is pretty straightforward. Greg dies, Susie gets the money, and they ride off into the sunset. Actually, I guess Susie's would be the same, but the sister? That's odd."

"Mike, do you know much about stun guns?"

"Probably more than the average person, and your friend Pete was right. The relatively new liquid stun gun is considered to be better in some instances because you have more shots and they can be fired from a greater distance. Whether that's what happened, I don't know."

"Won't the autopsy clear up some of this?"

"I'm banking on it. We should find out Greg's blood level from it, and we'll probably find out if a stun gun was used on Greg."

"I kind of thought the autopsy might show that, since there would have been an effect on his nervous system. Right?"

"I think so, Kelly, but I have to be honest with you. This is pretty new technology, and I'm not exactly certain how much of a stun gun's effect will show up in an autopsy."

"I take it you haven't heard any more from the coroner?"

"No, I thought I'd call him in the morning and see if he's been able to conduct the autopsy. I know today was probably tough for him with the DA and the press breathing down his neck, so I didn't want to add to his problems."

"That was thoughtful of you," Kelly said.

"Yep, that's me, the thoughtful sheriff. I was planning on talking to this Johnny guy tomorrow, you know, the personal trainer at the fitness center, but given what Pete told you, I think I'll wait to see what the coroner's report has to say."

"Mike, this is theoretical, but say the coroner's report comes back that Greg was hit with a stun gun and there's a very good chance that's what caused him to go overboard. Could you arrest Johnny for causing Greg's death?

"I've been thinking about it, and I see some huge problems with it. First of all, it was a new moon, a night when it's pretty much pitch dark, even though there would have been some stars in the sky. By Pete's own admission he couldn't clearly see the person who was in the kayak or what was on their back. He identified the man by his kayak and talk of who the kayak owner was not by visually seeing and identifying him."

"I think I see where this is going," Kelly said.

"I don't think there is any way Pete could identify Johnny as the man in the kayak. The next problem I have would be Greg's blood alcohol level. No matter what would happen with the stun gun, I think it's pretty safe to assume that Greg's blood alcohol level is going to be sky high and way over the legal limit. Any defense attorney worth his salt would use that as the reason Greg went overboard."

"Yes, I agree," Kelly said. "And I would imagine the fact that he had cancer would also be brought up. Probably that he was in a weakened condition, and that could have affected his balance."

"You're right, and we haven't even seen the autopsy report. What if Greg had a heart attack, and even if he was shot with a stun gun and it caused it, I think it would be impossible to tell if he had had the heart attack seconds before the jolt from the stun gun hit him or seconds after the stun gun. I think it would just show that he'd had a heart attack, and again, a defense attorney would certainly play that up."

"Okay, that's enough for tonight. Dinner will be served in ten minutes and we'll make it an early night. After the day you've had, I'm sure you could use a good night's sleep. Maybe a couple of television programs between dinner and bed, but no midnight surfing. Got it?"

"Yes, boss."

CHAPTER NINETEEN

Mike was exhausted after, what he felt, was a day that presented more questions than answers concerning the death of his friend, Greg. He kept going over and over the sequence of events that led to his death and couldn't come up with a plausible reason why his friend had fallen overboard.

"Tell you what, Mike, you just go to bed," Kelly said when they'd finished eating. "I'll let the dogs out and then I'll join you. I don't know why, but I'm really tired, too."

"I think it's this whole Greg thing, Kelly. I'm really struggling with believing that anyone would want to murder Greg, and particularly for money, but I have to say I'm leaning in that direction."

"I agree, but maybe like Doc said, it was a blessing in disguise. At least he didn't suffer, so there is that."

"Guess it kind of goes back to what I do and how I believe. A crime is a crime and to me, murder is right up there with the worst. Even if it saved Greg from suffering, it's still wrong, and on that note, I'll leave you. See you in the morning."

"Night, love. Things will look better in the morning."

"I know, Kelly. Your eternal optimism of the half full glass versus the half empty glass is making itself known, but right now the glass looks completely empty to me," he said as he walked down the hall to their bedroom.

"Rebel, Lady, Skyy, time to go outside. Come on," Kelly said as she opened the sliding door from the great room to the back yard. She walked out with them and looked out at the bay, thinking about Greg. *If the murderer was Johnny, had Susie known he was going to shoot Greg with the gun? Was she part of it? Had she texted him or done something to let him know when they'd be leaving the restaurant? Like Mike had said, there were simply too many unanswered questions.*

She brought the dogs in, gave them each a treat, and locked up the house. A few minutes later she was in bed and as sound asleep as Mike was. She was awakened several hours later by the ringing of Mike's cell phone. He was sleeping so soundly, he was completely unaware of it.

Kelly reached over him and grabbed the phone. Looking at the monitor, she saw the call was from Jessica. She answered it and said, "Jessica, I'll get Mike. Just a moment."

She put her hand over the phone, shook him, and said, "Mike, Mike, wake up. Jessica's on the phone." He instantly became awake and took the phone from her.

"Hi, Jess, sorry I didn't pick up. I went to bed early after a frustrating day. It's 1:30, what's up? Are you okay?"

He heard Jessica crying on the other end of the line and then she said tearfully, "Yes, I'm okay. Oh, Mike, this is awful."

"Take your time, Jess. I've got all night. Breathe deeply a couple of times and then tell me what's so awful."

She was quiet for several moments and then said, "Mike, do you know what a butt call is?"

"Yeah, I've received a couple and hate to say it, but I've also sent a couple. It happens when the button on someone's cell phone accidently activates and a phone call is made to the last number dialed on the phone. Often it's caused when someone sits on their phone. Thus, the phrase 'butt call.' What about them?"

"Well, I just got one. Excuse me, Mike, I need to say something to Mark." He heard her reassuring her husband that she was all right and was telling Mike what had happened.

She came back on the line and said, "Mike, about fifteen minutes ago my phone rang. I was in bed and didn't bother to look at the monitor. I was thinking if someone was calling this late, it was probably a real emergency. Cissy, one of my daughters, is staying at a friend's house tonight on a sleepover, so my first thought was that something had happened to her."

"Perfectly natural, Jess. Go on."

"Well, it had nothing to do with Cissy. It was a butt call from Scott, which, as you know, means it was an inadvertent call. That's not surprising, considering how many times he's called me in the last forty-eight hours."

"No, and I'm glad you're not taking those calls," Mike said.

"Yeah, well, I sure wish I hadn't answered this one."

"Something disturbing, I'm guessing?"

"Beyond. He and his wife, Nita, were talking about Dad's death. Scott was ranting and raving about how there was no way he could get the $100,000 in time for tomorrow's 10:00 a.m. deadline that Lem had given him. I guess Lem gave him an extra few hours from the time of Dad's death."

"That doesn't sound like anything new," Mike said.

"No, it wasn't, but here's the part that's new. Nita said, and I quote, because these words will be forever etched on my brain, 'Well, you and that ditsy wife of his agreed to get rid him by having her push him overboard. Only problem was she did it a day too late. If she'd done it a day earlier, you both would have gotten 1/3 of the estate and she would have gotten the $250,000 bonus you promised her for taking care of it, because you knew he was going to change his trust. He just beat you both to it. Now you're not gonna' get a thing.'"

"She went on to say that Scott was a loser and he couldn't even arrange for a slam dunk way to make a couple of million dollars. Nita said he should have insisted that Susie get Greg to go to the restaurant a day or two earlier. She said if he'd been more forceful, Scott would have gotten his money and Susie would have gotten her 1/3 plus the bonus."

"Oh, sweetheart, I am so sorry you had to hear that," Mike said.

Jessica began to sob and Mike could hear Mark talking to her. He held the phone and waited, knowing she'd come back on the phone when she'd gotten herself under control.

"Mike, I never want to see Scott or Susie again. Even though Scott is my brother, he's out of my life."

"I can understand why you feel that way. Jess, I was going to call you tomorrow to bring you up to date on a few things that happened today regarding your father's death. Even though Susie and Scott may have plotted together for her to push him overboard and drown, that may not be what actually happened.

"What I'm about to tell you doesn't make their actions any less despicable, but their actions may not have been what caused your father's death. Here's what Kelly and I found out today."

He spent the next half hour telling her about his meetings, Kelly's meeting, and the implication of what they had learned from these meetings. During the time she was listening to Mike, Jessica's attention was diverted from her father and Susie. In a few minutes, her voice had returned to normal as she asked Mike questions.

"Mike, what's next?" Jessica asked.

"I plan on going to Johnny's home in the morning. I called my deputy before I went to bed and had him get Johnny's address and his schedule at the fitness center for me. He's off tomorrow until noon. After that I'll get in touch with the coroner, and hopefully, his report will answer some of our questions."

"Mike would you do me a favor and call me after you talk to both of them?"

"Of course, Jess. That's about everything for now. I guess to sum it up, unless it comes back that your father simply had a natural heart attack, if there is such a thing, it looks like someone caused him to drown because of their actions. It could have been Johnny with the stun gun or it could have been Susie doing something in the boat.

"I want to leave you with one thought," Mike continued, "and I suppose it comes from that old phrase about making lemonade out of lemons. One of Kelly's regular customers, Doc Burkham, was in her coffee shop today and said something to her that you might want to think about."

"What was that?" Jess asked.

"He said maybe your father's drowning was a blessing…"

Jessica interrupted him. "Why would he say something stupid like that?"

"Hear me out, Jess. He said it might have been a blessing because given the type of cancer your father had, his last days would have been very painful, and at least he didn't have to go through that."

Jessica was quiet for several moments, and then said, "Mike, our family goes to church every Sunday. I always tell my girls that God has a bigger plan for us than we can possibly know. Well, maybe, just maybe, God had a bigger plan for my dad than I selfishly would have wanted. I would have wanted more time with him, but at what cost to him? I was putting my needs before his, and that was wrong."

"So thanks, Mike. I think I'll be able to sleep better from now on, no matter how this turns out. On that note, we both better get some sleep, and Mike, I can never thank you enough for what you're doing. You're a fine man and worthy to have been my father's best friend."

When the call had ended Mike looked over at Kelly, who had tears running down her cheeks. "I gather you heard our conversation."

"Oh, Mike, that poor little girl. I know she's an adult, but she'll always be daddy's girl. I think another good thing about all of this, if you can call it that, is that Greg will never have to know how his son betrayed him. If he had known, that alone might have killed him."

"Knowing Greg as I did, I think it would have. Go back to sleep, Kelly. Love you," Mike said as he turned off the light.

CHAPTER TWENTY

When Mike woke up the next morning, Kelly had already left for the coffee shop. He walked into the kitchen and found a note on the counter from Kelly.

"Mike, thought you needed to sleep in after last night. Dogs have been fed, the coffee's ready for you, and there are some of those cinnamon rolls I made for Cash yesterday in the frig. Just heat them up in the microwave. Today's newspaper's underneath this note. Might take a look at the article about a woman named Kendra. Looks a lot like Susie. Good luck today. Loves and see you tonight."

He smiled thinking how very Kelly that note was. Kelly and her food. She always wanted to make sure that everyone was well fed. He got a treat for each of the dogs who had been sitting next to the pantry door where the treats were kept in anticipation of Mike's morning ritual – starting his day out by giving each of them a treat.

Mike poured himself a cup of coffee and spread the newspaper out. "What the…" he said as he looked at the headline in The Oregonian. In bold print were the words "Kendra James Arrested for Embezzling Senior Citizens Funds."

He took a long sip of coffee and began to read the article. When he was finished, he sat back, thought about what he'd just read, and then re-read the article in its entirety. He spent a long time looking at the picture of the woman, the woman who was Susie's sister, the woman he and Cash had met only days before.

According to the article in the newspaper, Kendra was the bookkeeper for a large company that owned a number of assisted living homes in Oregon. Through an investigation that had lasted several months, it was determined that she had embezzled over $750,000 from the company, primarily funds that had been paid to the company by senior citizens for help in their twilight years.

The paper went on to say that she was in custody and was to be arraigned today on charges of embezzlement. The District Attorney said with the amount of evidence the investigators had found, Ms. James would be in prison much longer than the people she had stolen from would be alive.

Even though Mike realized what the paper was saying about the predicted length of her time in prison, he thought it could have been worded a little better. Didn't sound very politically correct to him. However, being in law enforcement and dealing with the media multiple times both in print and television, he was well aware of the creed they lived by, "If it bleeds, it leads." And he had to agree, if the story had been written in a softer manner, it might not have been as effective or attention getting.

What a pair Kendra and Susie are. One embezzles and the other one makes a deal to essentially murder her husband. Nice job their parents did with them, he thought. *Wonder if they're alive to see the fruits of their labor?*

Mike thought about calling Kelly and telling her who Kendra was, but decided he'd tell her tonight. He looked at his watch and realized it was time to shower and dress if he was going to get to Johnny's house before Johnny left to run errands and go to work.

He walked into the bedroom, dogs following, and took a clean uniform out of the closet. After he'd finished with Johnny, he needed to go to the station and check on things there. He decided he'd call the coroner when he got to the station.

When he had his uniform on, and he'd put on his holster with the gun in it, Rebel came over and stood next to him. As Rebel had gotten older, Mike had started taking him to the station with him, and occasionally, on a call. Rebel had been a drug agent's dog before he was murdered, and as such, thoroughly trained to be a police dog. No matter what the situation, Mike always felt a little better when Rebel was around, so he decided to take him with him today.

Mike put Rebel in the back seat of his car, got into the front seat, plugged Johnny's address into his GPS, and began driving to it. As he got closer to the destination indicated by the GPS, he recognized the area from a drug case he'd been involved in a few years earlier.

It was in one of the older parts of Cedar Bay, an area where people who could afford to had moved to a more upscale house or apartment. The rents in the area where Johnny lived were low. He pulled up in front of a rundown apartment building and parked.

"Rebel, I'm going to take you in with me. Don't anticipate any trouble, since this is more like a meet and greet, but I kind of like to know you have my back, just in case." He opened the back door and attached Rebel's leash to his collar.

As they walked up the cracked sidewalk with weeds growing in the cracks, Mike watched Rebel. He was on full alert. Mike didn't know what was triggering it, but there was definitely something in the immediate area that Rebel didn't like.

When Mike got to the entrance of the two-story apartment, he saw a tenant roster next with a doorbell next to each name and an intercom. He rang the doorbell next to Johnny Larson's name and a moment later a male voice said, "Who is it?"

"It's Sheriff Mike Reynolds. I'm looking for Johnny Larson. I'd like to talk to him for a few minutes. It won't take long."

"I'm Johnny Larson. What's this about?" Johnny asked.

"The death of Greg Tuttle."

"All right," Johnny said in a calm voice. "I'm buzzing you in now. Open the door. Walk down the hall, and my apartment is the last one on the right."

Mike opened the door and he and Rebel walked down the hall. When he got to the end of the hall, a very muscular attractive man in a skintight black t-shirt and sweat pants, who he assumed was Johnny Larson, was waiting for him.

He looked down at Rebel and said, "You didn't tell me you had a dog. We have a very strict 'No Pet' policy here. You'll have to take him out and put him in your car."

Mike didn't know how many words Rebel knew, but he could definitely sense that Rebel didn't like Johnny. The hair along his back and his neck was raised, and Mike knew from experience that Rebel was on guard.

"Sorry, Johnny, he's a police dog. The rules that owners post about no pets allowed don't apply to police and service dogs. Anyway, we won't be long."

"Well, in that case, come on in," he said, gesturing towards his apartment. He walked in first and Mike and Rebel followed. The apartment was small, but well kept-up. No dirty dishes littered the kitchen counter or the sink, which in Mike's experience in dealing with single men who lived in apartments, was unusual.

"Have a seat," Johnny said. "You said you were here regarding Greg Tuttle's death. What would you like from me?"

"I understand that Greg Tuttle and his wife belong to the fitness center where you work. Do you know them?"

"Yes. I met Mr. Tuttle several times. He stopped coming to the fitness center, but his wife comes three times a week. Actually, I'm her personal trainer."

"I'm curious. How does the fitness center determine which trainer works with which client?"

"Usually it's kind of a round robin thing. In other words, it's the trainer who's next up in line. There are two other possibilities. First, if a client is a walk-in and wants someone right then to work with them, it will be whichever trainer is at the center and free to take a client.

"The other possibility is if a client requests a certain trainer," Johnny said with a smug look on his face.

"And how did you come to have Mrs. Tuttle as your client?" Mike asked as he reached down to pet Rebel who was still on alert.

"She chose me. I kind of have a reputation among the women, if you know what I mean," he said with a wink, "of being a good trainer."

"I see," Mike said. "How is she doing since her husband's death?"

"I don't know, I haven't seen her. Guess she'll be on easy street now that she's a rich widow."

"What makes you say that?" Mike asked, thinking that Johnny must not have heard about the terms of Greg's trust. He must have been telling the truth about not having seen Susie.

"C'mon, Sheriff. I mean everyone knew the guy was bucks up. They lived in that fancy house on the bay, she's dripping in jewels, and she drives a new Lexus. You don't need to be a rocket scientist to know that she's going to be sitting in some sweet clover."

"Yeah, I can sure see where someone would think that. Johnny, you look like you're very physically fit. What do you do to stay in such good shape?"

"Thanks, but you know, if you're gonna' be in this game, you better look like you can play. I do all kinds of workouts at the center, about an hour and a half a day. Plus, I'm really big into kayaking in the bay."

"I've heard that's very good for upper body strength. Any truth to it?" Mike asked.

"Sure is. Plus, just one hour of kayaking can burn over 350 calories, depending on how hard you paddle, and I paddle hard. I'm kind of a glutton for punishment, but it lets me eat pretty much whatever I want."

Mike looked out into the small patio area of Johnny's apartment and saw a kayak. "Is that your kayak?" he asked.

"Sure is. Sometimes I tie it up at the Cedar Bay public dock, but usually I bring it back here."

"Mind if I take a look at it? I don't know anything about kayaks. Wouldn't mind you giving me a lesson."

"Not a prob," Johnny said, sliding the glass door to the patio open. "Come on out."

He spent the next five minutes explaining why he'd chosen this particular kayak, ending with pointing out the white glow strips on the bow and the stern.

"I put them on the bow and the stern, because I often have to work all day and I can't get out on the bay until it's dark. In the winter, there aren't many boats on it, and I feel pretty safe.

"Summertime is a different story, though. We get all these people who haven't been on the water all year, and they're crazy. Half the time they're drunk when they're driving at night, so that's why I put them there. People can easily see them," Johnny said.

"That was smart. Do most kayakers do something like that so they don't get run over by a boat?"

"No, and I've always thought that was odd. I think I'm the only one who has a kayak on the bay with anything like that. My kayak is really one of a kind. It's unique, the only one like it around here."

"Well thanks for your time, Johnny. Appreciate the tutorial on your kayak. We'll be leaving. You probably have some things to do, and I don't want to take up all of your morning."

They went back into the small apartment and Mike and Rebel walked over to the front door. Mike turned back and said, "Thanks for seeing me." By the time they'd walked down the apartment hall, Rebel's hackles were back to normal, and it was as if he'd never been on alert.

Interesting, Mike thought. *I need to get in touch with Pete and see what he can tell me about those white glow strips. If they're that unique, and Johnny seemed to think they were, that might be hard to refute in court. I'll call Kelly from the station and get his phone number.*

CHAPTER TWENTY-ONE

"Good morning, Josh, thanks for covering for me."

"Sorry your vacation didn't work out so well, Sheriff, but we're always glad to see you. How are you doing as trustee of the Tuttle trust?"

"It's taken some real twists and turns. Let me tell you what's happened." He walked over and closed the door, sat down across the desk from Josh, Rebel at his feet, and filled him in on what he'd learned.

"Now I understand why you wanted Johnny Larson's information. By the way, Sheriff, I'm an avid kayaker and everyone knows that the kayak with the white glow strips on the bow and the stern is Johnny's."

"That's interesting. One more notch in a case that very well may be on the verge of being solved. I need to talk to Pete and see if he saw any glow strips on the kayak that night. I'm going into my office to call him. When I'm finished, I'll let you know what he says, then I need to call the coroner." Mike stood up and said, "Come," to Rebel who followed him out the door, down the hall, and into Mike's office.

A moment later he heard Roxie's familiar voice on the phone.

"Good morning, Roxie, it's Mike. Is my lovely wife available?"

"Available and standing right here. I'll put her on."

"Hi, sweetheart. What did you think of the newspaper article I left for you?" Kelly asked.

"Pretty ironic timing, Kelly. Kendra is Susie's sister. Remember, I met her at Susie's. Guess she doesn't have to worry about Susie living with her now. According to the paper, she'll be going away for a long time. And if we can find enough evidence against Susie, maybe they could be cellmates."

"Wow, that's a thought. I thought there was something familiar about her, but I just couldn't put my finger on it."

"As usual, your instincts were right on. Anyway, I had an interesting conversation with Johnny Larson a little while ago. He's Susie's personal fitness trainer and the one we've heard she's having an affair with. He certainly fits the image – very handsome and very muscular. He said something that I need to check out with Pete. Do you have his telephone number handy?"

"Yes, it's in my contacts list but let me call you right back. A couple of customers just walked in, and Roxie has her hands full with orders. Be just a minute," she said as she ended the call.

His phone rang two minutes later and it was Kelly. "Here's the number," she said as she recited it to him. "He mentioned he was going to be on a run today, but this is his cell number, so you should be able to reach him. You've whetted my curiosity. Tell me all about it tonight. Any word from the coroner?"

"No, when I finish with Pete, I plan on calling him. You better get back to work. I can hear a lot of commotion and in a coffee shop that's good. Means there's plenty of customers. Loves."

He tapped the numbers Kelly had given him on his cell phone and a moment later he heard a voice say, "Pete, here. What can I do for you?"

"Pete, it's Sheriff Reynolds. Got a minute to talk?"

"Sure do. I'm just rollin' down the highway, so a distraction would be welcome."

"First of all, I want to thank you for going to the coffee shop and telling Kelly about Johnny Larson. This is in regards to him. I just came from his apartment. I wanted to see what he'd say about Susie and Greg. There was nothing there, but what I did find interesting was his kayak. He gave me a tutorial on it. Can you think of anything distinctive about it?"

"Yes, and I think I neglected to mention this to Kelly. His kayak has white glow strips on the bow and the stern. It's very distinctive. As a matter of fact, I've never seen another one like it. They glow in the dark, and I did notice them when the kayak passed in front of me the night Greg died. I don't know why I didn't say anything to Kelly. Sorry."

"Don't be. Your conversation with her led me to him and there was a white glow strip on the bow and another one on the stern of his kayak which he had stored on his patio. You're on the water a lot and if you think it's something that sets his kayak apart from others, I'll take your word for it. He told me it was pretty distinctive. I'm going to call my friend Jack over at his marine repair shop and see if he knows of another one like that."

"Make you a bet, Sheriff."

"I'm not much of a gambler, but I've been known to take a bet or two. What's the bet?"

"Bet you a six-pack of beer that Johnny, think that's the name you used, is the only one who's on the bay in a kayak with those glow in the dark type of strips."

"My friend, that's a bet I'm not going to take, because I'm sure you're right. Thanks again for your information and drive safe."

"Will do. Go get the bad guys."

"I'm trying, Pete, believe me, I'm trying."

CHAPTER TWENTY-TWO

"This is Sheriff Reynolds," Mike said to the young man who answered the phone at the marine repair shop. "I'd like to speak with Jack, if he's around."

"Gonna' take a couple of minutes, Sheriff, he's out on the dock giving an estimate. Might be easier if he called you back."

"That's fine," Mike said, "here's my number." He ended the call and looked at the phone.

Might as well call the coroner and see what he's found out, Mike thought.

He pressed the coroner's phone number into his cell phone and a woman's voice said, "County Coroner's Office, how may I direct your call?"

"This is Sheriff Reynolds. I'd like to speak with the coroner. Is he available?"

"Not at the moment, sir. He's just finishing up an autopsy. I could have him call you back in about half an hour."

"Sure. I'd appreciate it. He has my number," Mike said.

A moment later his secretary said, "Jack's Marine Repair is on line one returning your call, Sheriff."

"Thanks, Betty. I'll take it."

"Hi, Jack. Appreciate you getting back to me so fast."

"No problem, Mike. I just stand in awe of the messes these, we call 'em 'baby boaters,' can get into when they come to the coast and put their boats in the water for the first time. You know, Oregon has a mandatory boating safety class that owners have to take if they're going to operate a boat that has an engine with more than 10 horsepower, but I think a lot of them flake on it. That, or they buy their boat from an individual, and they don't take the class at all."

"I didn't know that about the course. Makes sense."

"Yeah, typical bureaucrat good idea. Looks great on paper, but the implementation is something else. Oh well, like I said the other day, that's what pays for my son's medical school and my daughter's law school. Now, what can I help you with?"

"Jack, ever heard of anyone doing something to their kayak to make it safe for use at night?"

"That's a rather convoluted question, Sheriff, but I think I know where you're going with it. I only know one person who has done something like that. His name is Johnny Larson. He has a kayak he takes out on the bay pretty much every night. Instead of having running lights on it, or something like that, he put white glow strips on the bow and the stern. You can always see him when you're in the water at night."

"So you don't know anyone else who has a kayak like his?"

"No, and sooner or later, just about everything connected with boating winds up in my shop. Johnny's kayak is one of a kind. Quite unusual, but in a way, brilliant. Even the baby boaters steer clear of him when he's out in the bay at night. Anything else?"

"One more question just occurred to me. Are there many kayakers that use the bay?"

"No, actually there are very few. I think kayaks are kind of a trendy thing. I've seen photographs of people in their kayaks in the waters around Portland, San Francisco, and Los Angeles. Whenever I see one, I think how glad I am I live in Cedar Bay, so I don't have to get caught up in the latest trend or fad.

"We're kind of a conservative little town without a lot of young people trying out the latest thing. You know, we're mostly a bunch of retired people who are set in our ways. Anyway, I've only seen a couple of kayaks out on the waters of Cedar Bay."

"Thanks Jack, you've answered my questions. Appreciate your help."

"Sheriff, I happened to be working late the night Greg drowned. Don't know where you're at with Johnny, but I saw his kayak on the water that night. I have a bad habit of using my binoculars from time to time to check out what's going on out in the bay. Since so many of the boats out on the bay end up here in my shop, figure I'm just preparing myself in case one of them gets in trouble."

"What time did you see Johnny's kayak, Jack?"

"About five minutes before the Coast Guard arrived at the location where Greg fell out of the boat. If you're going to ask me if I saw it after the Coast Guard and everyone left, I'd have to say no, but by then Johnny wasn't on my radar."

"Again, thanks."

"Good luck with whatever it is you're doing," Jack said as he ended the call.

CHAPTER TWENTY-THREE

A moment after Mike ended the call with Jack, his phone rang. He picked it up and said, "Yes, Betty?"

"Sheriff, it's Leo, over at the coroner's office returning your call."

"Good, thanks. I'll take it."

"Good afternoon, Leo. I'm not pressing you because I know you had the shooting on the other side of the county, but I was wondering if you had anything for me on the Greg Tuttle autopsy."

"I just finished it, Sheriff. It's one of the more interesting autopsies I've ever done."

"In what way?" Mike asked.

"Not just in one way, but in several ways. Here we go. I assume you know that Greg Tuttle had cancer, a very advanced form of pancreatic cancer."

"Yes, he told me about it the last time I saw him just before he died."

"This part is a bit delicate, because I've heard he was your best friend, and you're also the trustee of his trust."

"Leo, I have a feeling there's something really off here, so the time for delicacies has passed," Mike said.

"Okay. The decedent had a blood alcohol level of 1.8. As you know, Sheriff, that's over twice what the legal limit is here in Oregon."

"Yeah, Leo, I was afraid of that. I'm not surprised. I've been investigating this and was pretty sure that's what you'd say."

"Sheriff, his daughter has called me several times, and as his daughter, she has a right to know what his blood alcohol level was. There is no legal reason for me not to tell her other than I hate doing something like this, since girls often look up to their dads, and don't want to hear unpleasant things like this."

"That's very perceptive of you, Leo, but there's no reason she shouldn't know, hard as it may be for her to accept the fact that her father was severely intoxicated. She's had some other pretty tough knocks in the last couple of days, and I wish there was some way to prevent her from finding out, but there's nothing I can do about it."

"All right. I wanted to check with you before I talked to her. I'll call her back when we're finished."

"Okay. What about a heart attack? Any evidence of that?" Mike asked.

"No, and believe me, I really looked for signs of that, because to just go overboard, even with a high alcohol level in the body, and not struggle to be saved is really odd. I thought a heart attack might be the cause of death, but it wasn't."

"What are you putting down as the cause of death?"

"Greg Tuttle died from drowning. Quite frankly, he suffocated because of submersion in the waters of the bay. There were definite signs of his body being deprived of oxygen which damaged his organs, particularly the lungs and the brain."

"Obviously, given the fact that when the Coast Guard brought him out of the water, he was dead, I'm not at all surprised that you found that to be the cause of death," Mike said.

"Yes, but Sheriff, there is something else that I think contributed to his death."

"What would that be, Leo?"

"This is something I've not dealt with before, and only read about, but I think the decedent was the victim of a stun gun being fired at him before he fell in the water and drowned."

"What makes you say that?"

"What I saw is consistent with what I've read. You see when someone is repeatedly shocked with more than the 100 millivolts the human body generates on its own, an electrical response like a power surge is sent to their nerves. The shock overwhelms the nervous system and causes the muscles to lock up. Greg Tuttle's muscles were locked up."

"Leo, can you think of any other reason the muscles would be locked up?"

"A spinal cord injury would be the most common way that all of the body's muscles would lock up, but there were no signs of a spinal cord injury."

"So, what you're saying is that the injuries to his muscles were consistent with being hit by an electrical charge from a stun gun."

"Yes, that's what I'm saying based on what I've read. I've never done an autopsy on someone who has had a stun gun or a taser used on thim, so I'm basing this on intellectual knowledge, not firsthand knowledge."

"I see. Let me reiterate what I think you're saying, and please, correct me if I'm wrong. What I'm hearing is that Greg Tuttle died from drowning. He was suffering from advanced cancer. And the reason he may have fallen overboard and drowned is due to having his muscles locked up because of being hit by an electrical charge from a stun gun or a taser.

"Because of his muscles locking up, he was incapacitated and unable to try to save himself, and thus he drowned. Is that about it?"

"Yes, that all fits with what I saw when I examined the body."

"Thanks, Leo. I appreciate the fine work you've done. I do have one request."

"What's that?"

"I'd appreciate it if you didn't tell his daughter about the stun gun theory at this point. I personally think it's far more than a theory, but right now I think it would be easier for her to accept that her father drowned, rather than think that someone might have murdered him."

"I understand, and I agree. From what you're saying, I assume you have reason to believe he was murdered."

"I do, but I also realize trying to prove it, given what we have, may be very difficult. I need to check out a few more things."

"Sheriff, as I told you, this is pretty new territory for me. If I have to go to court in this case, I want you to know up front that I couldn't say with absolute certainty that Greg Tuttle drowned because he was hit with a stun gun or taser and that's what caused him to go into the water. I want to be very clear about that so you don't base your case on my testimony."

"I completely understand, and I appreciate your honesty."

"Sheriff, now you can do me a favor."

"Sure, if I can, I'd be happy to."

"Call me and let me know how this goes down. I'm very curious about the ultimate outcome. Not only intellectually, but also emotionally."

"Consider it done, and again, thanks for your time."

CHAPTER TWENTY-FOUR

Mike spent the next few hours working at the station and at 5:30 he said, "Rebel, we've had a full day. Think I need to go home and bounce all of this off Kelly. Let's go."

Mike was pretty sure that one of Rebel's operative words was "go," because whenever he said it, Rebel was up and looking at Mike for his next command.

He'd taken Rebel with him to the station enough times that when they returned home Lady and Skyy weren't jealous, just curious about where Rebel had been. They spent the next few minutes sniffing him, and then satisfied, went over to the pantry door where the dog cookies were kept, expecting their evening treat. Mike complied.

"All right, Sheriff, now that the important stuff is done, like giving the dogs their evening treats, how about a hug for your wife?"

"You got it, Kelly," he said as he gave her a big hug. "I'm going to change clothes and take off my sheriff's hat, literally. Back in a few minutes."

"Mike, it's really warm here in the kitchen. I've got a roast in the oven, and it's heating up the room as well. I made a big batch of lemonade. I'm going to have a glass and enjoy the view of the bay from the patio. Care to join me?"

"That sounds great. I'll pour the lemonade while you finish whatever you're working on. Meet you out there."

A few minutes later they were sitting at the patio table, petting the dogs, and enjoying the view. "You know, Kelly, I'm having a hard time looking at Greg's house now that he's gone. We've always looked down there to see if they were home or whatever, but now it hurts."

"I know, honey. That's always the first thing I did whenever I came out here as well. I mean, just now when we walked out I did it, noticed that all was quiet and thought that was about right, since Greg's no longer there. By the way, as trustee, what are you going to do about Susie living in the house?"

"I've been holding off on everything until the time passed for Scott to pay his money to the trust, but it's now past the time required. Lem told me that Greg had told him he'd like to see Susie out of the house within a few days of the date of his death. Evidently he was concerned that she might do something to damage the house because he knew she'd be angry about Greg changing the trust."

"From what we've found out about her, I wouldn't put it past her."

"Nor would I. That's on my list of things to do tomorrow, and to say I'm looking forward to it would be a gross overstatement."

"Did you get a chance to talk to Pete today?"

"I did, and Jack, and Johnny, and the coroner. How long do we have until dinner?"

"About an hour. Why?" Kelly asked

"Just didn't want to ruin dinner talking about my day while the roast burned. I want to fill you in on those conversations and get your take, but it may take a little while."

When he'd finished telling her about his conversations, she sat back and said, "Looks like Johnny's responsible for Greg's death. In other words, he murdered him. Odd way to do it, but the result was the same as if he'd used a gun or a knife."

"Sure is my conclusion, but proving it is going to be difficult. Talk about circumstantial evidence. I probably have enough to arrest him, but unless he owned up to doing it, there is simply not enough evidence for the District Attorney to make a case against him. As sure as I am he murdered Greg, all I really have is speculation. I don't have Johnny holding the smoking gun, so to speak. That's the bottom line."

"Mike, you've had several tough days. The roast should be done by now. It's such a beautiful night, let's eat out here. Okay with you?"

"Sounds great. I'll set the table while you get the food. Actually, looking into the eyes of these three dogs, better put feeding them on my list as well."

*****

"That was a terrific meal, Kelly. I swear, sometimes there is nothing better than a good old roast, some little roasted potatoes, carrots, and gravy. Probably not going to help my weigh-in tomorrow, but it was worth every bite."

"I agree. Sit here while I clear the dishes. Join me in a brandy out here? It's such a beautiful night, and since we're at the end of summer, I'd like to make it last a little longer."

"Great idea, but let me help you clear the dishes. You've worked hard all day, too."

"Okay, guys, just don't tell her," Mike said as he carried the remains of the roast into the kitchen and gave each of the dogs several pieces. He was sure he could stand there for hours giving them pieces of meat, and they'd never indicate they'd had enough.

"You know, Mike, even given the events of the last few days, we really are lucky to live here. My parents did a good thing fifty years ago when they bought this piece of land and built on it. We've got one of the best views of the bay and if we were boaters, we could walk down all those steps to our boat."

"The view, the house, the land, I agree are fabulous. Walking down to the dock has never excited me, but I'm sure if and when we sell this house, it would probably make this property even more desirable. Who knows? Some really wealthy person could install an elevator. If I had the money, I might do that myself," Mike said.

"Yeah, but then you'd have to get a boat, and then you have to… Mike, the list would go on and on. Right?" She waited for a moment, but there was no response from Mike. "Mike?" she said again.

"Sorry, Kelly, but I'm seeing some activity at Greg's house. Looks like Susie, and believe it or not, Johnny, are sitting down at the table on the deck and having a glass of wine. I'm going to go in the house and get our binoculars."

He returned a moment later and looked down at the deck outside the Tuttle house.

"Well, is it them?" Kelly asked.

"Sure is. Seems a little blatant, doesn't it? I mean Greg's only been gone a couple of days, and she's sitting on Greg's deck with her lover. Wonder what they're talking about? How he killed Greg? I can't stand this. I'm going down there," Mike said as he walked back in the house.

Kelly hurried after him. "Wait, Mike. What are you going to do when you get down there?"

"I don't know. I'll play it by ear, but I'm darned sure going to take my gun." He strode down the hall and returned a minute later with a jacket covering his holster and gun.

"Mike, don't do anything rash. Think as a sheriff, not as a friend. Just listen and see if you can pick up something. I want Rebel to go with you. If something happens, we know he'll help. I'd like to come, too."

"No, I don't want you to come. It could be dangerous You stay up here and watch what happens. If you see that I'm in trouble, call Josh. He can have a deputy there in a couple of minutes." He turned to the dogs. "Rebel, let's go."

They went into the garage and a minute later, Kelly heard his car start and the garage door go down. She hurried back to the patio and picked up the binoculars. She watched Mike's car as it went down the hill and then lost it when he was on the road that circled the bay and led to the Tuttle house.

CHAPTER TWENTY-FIVE

"Johnny, I don't think this was a good idea. After all, I'm supposed to be a grieving widow," Susie said.

Mike could hear perfectly from where he'd concealed himself behind the wooden fence that abutted the deck of the Tuttle's home. He gave the "stay" hand signal to Rebel, who was sitting at his feet, waiting for a command.

"Don't be silly, Susie. You're simply having a glass of wine with your personal trainer who came here to pay his respects to Greg. That's pretty innocent, and I doubt it would offend anyone."

"I don't know, Johnny, maybe we should lie low for a while."

"Susie, now that you have all that money, you can do whatever you want, and no one is going to say anything. That's the way it is with wealthy people. They're immune to what other people think."

"Johnny, there's a lot you don't know. I'm as responsible for Greg's death as you are. After all, I made sure that the drinks kept coming at the restaurant that night, and even though Greg probably appeared sober, I know he was drunk. Greg could always hide it well. I've told everyone that he was the one who drove the boat home, that he stood up, must have become dizzy, and then fell overboard."

"But Johnny, that's not what really happened. I was driving the boat when we left the restaurant. I knew you were waiting out on the bay somewhere to shoot Greg with the stun gun you bought, but I didn't know exactly where you were located.

"I was driving the boat as fast as it would go, even though there's a 5 mile per hour speed limit in the bay after dark. I figured if I couldn't locate you, I'd just try and push Greg over the side. He was so drunk, I thought it would be easy.

"Anyway, when I got the boat going quite fast, Greg stood up from where he was sitting in the front of the boat and moved to the back of the boat and stood beside me. He told me I was going too fast, and I'd get a citation from the Coast Guard if I didn't slow down. He was staggering and wobbly on his feet, and he nearly fell down when he was standing next to me. I figured it would be the perfect time for me to make a sharp turn with the boat, which would cause Greg to lose his balance.

"When that happened, it would be easy enough for me to simply give him a little shove and over the side he'd go. Just as I was getting ready to make the sharp turn, his whole body suddenly became stiff and rigid and he fell overboard like a downed timber. That must have been when you shot him with the stun gun.

"After he went over the side, I just kept going with the boat and didn't stop. Even if Greg sobered up and tried to save himself, he wouldn't be able to because the boat wasn't anywhere near him. I drove the boat around in several big circles, cried out for help, and then eventually I crashed the boat into another boat that was moored at a nearby dock. That made the whole thing look like some kind of a terrible accident."

"Susie, don't think about what you and I did. You got your money and now you and I can lead the life we've talked about. We can leave Cedar Bay and go wherever you want," Johnny said.

"But Johnny, you don't understand. Greg changed his trust and signed it on the day he died. If we'd been a day earlier, I would have gotten 1/3 of his estate. Now I'm only going to get a measly 10%."

"What? He changed his trust before we had a chance to kill him?" Johnny shouted. "You told me he was going to do that, but I thought it was way down the line."

"No, like I said, he signed it the morning he died. I didn't know he'd changed it or I would have never gone ahead with our plan to kill him. We killed him for practically nothing. We'll be lucky to live a couple of months on what he left me. Now I'm a murderer, and I have to live with the fact that I committed murder for peanuts."

"So am I," Johnny said. "So am I."

Mike's ears perked up. He was wishing he'd brought his phone so he could record the conversation when he felt a hand on his arm. He swung the gun around at the same time that Rebel growled.

Jack from the marine repair shop held his hands up and mouthed "Don't Shoot." Mike quizzically looked at him. Jack leaned into him and whispered in his ear, "I heard everything. Let's listen."

"What are you talking about, Johnny?"

"I wanted us to be together, and we needed that money," Johnny said. "I knew you and Greg went to the restaurant almost every night, and I've seen you come home from there enough times when I've been in my kayak that I came up with the idea to shoot him with a stun gun and make it look like an accidental drowning by a man that had too much to drink.

"I shot him with a liquid stun gun. It's a pretty new thing that allows a shooter to quickly take multiple shots. When I saw him standing beside you in the boat, that's when I let him have it. Gave him three quick bursts from the stun gun and it worked like a charm. You saw the results. It worked perfectly.

"When I saw that Greg was incapacitated in the water, I made a beeline back to the dock. Halfway back to the dock, I stopped in the middle of the bay and threw the stun gun and my backpack over the side. The bay is sixty feet deep there and no one will ever find them, so they can't be used as evidence against me.

"After I shot him, the next thing I knew you'd taken off in the inflatable. People were responding to your cries for help and trying to help, but it was no use. Greg's muscles had seized up and he was dead weight in the water. That's why it took the Coast Guard so long to bring him up out of the water."

"Oh, Johnny, what now? If anyone finds out what we did, we could both be tried for murder. And I didn't even get the money I was supposed to get," Susie wailed.

"I'll tell you what's next," Mike said as he stepped out from behind the fence where he had been hiding, Rebel next to him, gun in hand. "What's next is I arrest both of you for the murder of Greg Tuttle. I have a witness who heard everything the two of you just said."

At that moment, Jack stepped up beside him. Mike continued, "Don't either of you think about running, because not only is there nowhere to go, but Rebel would be more than happy to take you to the ground and leave a love bite that will probably never heal. And that's assuming he doesn't go for your jugular vein while he's at it."

"You haven't got anything on me," Johnny said. "I just came here to pay my condolences to Susie. There's no way you can prove that I was involved in Mr. Tuttle's death. I want to call my attorney."

"Me, too," Susie said. "You have no proof whatsoever that I was involved in his death."

"You can call an attorney once you get to the station. Jack, I see you have a cell phone. I forgot mine. Would you call this number?" Mike asked and handed him a card. "And then hand me your phone."

A moment later, Mike said, "This is Sheriff Reynolds. I need men and cars at the address I'm going to give you ASAP. I have two suspects in the Greg Tuttle drowning in custody."

Within minutes the sound of sirens filled the air. Sheriff's deputies fanned out on the deck while Johnny and Susie proclaimed their innocence. When they both had been handcuffed, Rebel laid down and watched everyone, paying particular attention to what Mike was doing.

When the sheriff's deputies had left with Susie and Johnny, and it was quiet, Mike turned to Jack and said, "Jack, why are you here?"

"I was on my way home. I live just two blocks down the street from here. I know this is the Tuttle's house, and I saw Johnny's car in the driveway along with yours. Johnny has a distinctive car. Not too many red Camaros in Cedar Bay. Think it's probably the only one. Anyway, given our recent conversations, I didn't like the idea of the three of you here. Thought I'd drop in and see if I could help. After all, what are friends for?"

"Well, let's put it this way. A friend who happens to drop in and overhear the conversations that will result in some guilty people going to prison are the kind of friends I want to have. Having both of us testify as to what we heard should seal a conviction for the District Attorney."

"Happy to be of service. You know I was thinking, Mike. You've got a really big dock. Sure would be a nice place for a big boat, don't you think?"

"No, I don't think," Mike said with a laugh. "Not gonna' happen. Why don't you follow me up to my house and join Kelly and me for a celebratory glass of brandy?"

"Make it wine and you're on. I haven't eaten yet and brandy before dinner doesn't sound all that great."

"Wine we have. Might even have some leftover roast, too, if you're interested," Mike said as they walked out to their cars.

EPILOGUE – TWO MONTHS LATER

"Mike, I just got a text from Cash and he can get leave in a month. If that timing is okay with you, he said he'd go ahead and make the reservations again for Kauai."

"That's fine with me. Fall's a good time for me to get away because the summer vacationers are gone and it's usually a little slower at that time of year. Plus, since I never used those vacation days when we were going to go, I'm fine with that. Shoot him back a text and tell him it works for us, and we're really looking forward to it."

Kelly was quiet for a few minutes as she pressed the keys on her cell phone, then she looked up at Mike and said, "Done. And I'm so glad it's going to work out. I was sorry we had to cancel on Cash when Greg died, but given the circumstances, we really didn't have a choice."

"Agreed. By the way, I got a phone call from Jessica today, and everything's going well with her. I had sent a cashier's check to her for the sale of the house. She really lucked out with the buyer. Not too many people want to buy a house with a thirty-day escrow and pay cash. That's one less thing she has to worry about."

"How do you think she's doing, Mike? I know she and her father were very close and with everything that happened, a lot of people in her situation would be spending a sizable chunk of their inheritance on therapy."

"She sounded very good. We're really ticking off the things that needed to be done to close the trust. I've been able to sell almost everything with the exception of the house in Palm Springs, but that's only because she decided she wants to keep it."

"Has she heard from Scott?" Kelly asked.

"She told me she opened a text from him. It was a copy of a text that Nita had sent him in which she told him he was a loser and she was leaving him. Then he wrote Jess his life had completely fallen apart, and it was all her fault."

"How did she take it?"

"She said she's finally seeing him for what he is. She said her father saw it a long time ago, but she kept convincing her dad to do things for Scott because he was her dad's son and her brother. She said if she had to do it all over again, she'd have agreed with her father. Maybe if Greg hadn't rescued Scott so often, he would have turned out to be an honorable person."

"Yes, and then again maybe not. I think there are just some bad seeds born into the world, and he's one. I'm not sure Greg could have done anything to make a difference. You know, kind of like we're our children's caretakers for a while and then that's it. Goes back to the old debate of hereditary versus environment."

"That's not one debate I'm getting into with you. Think that's a no winner, because no one knows for certain."

"I agree, so Scott's out of the picture. In his text Cash asked what happened to Susie and Johnny. What is happening with them?"

"They've both been charged with murder and their trials will be coming up in the next few months, barring attempts from their attorneys to delay them, which is a pretty common tactic defense attorneys use to drag these things out forever."

"Do you think they'll both be convicted and go to prison, Mike?"

"I think the DA will have a pretty good case against Johnny. After I overheard him say he'd dumped the stun gun and backpack in the bay, we used an underwater camera to try and find it. We were successful and when we got it to the lab for analysis, it had Johnny's fingerprints all over it. That evidence, plus the confession that Jack and I overheard him make when he told Susie that he shot Greg multiple times with the stun gun, should be enough to convict him.

"I don't know about Susie. The case against her will be difficult to prove. Sure, we have my testimony and Jack's about what we heard her say, but with Johnny being the actual shooter and her only involvement being getting Greg drunk, it could be dicey. I suppose a lot of it will depend on how much of Johnny's involvement the judge will allow to be used against her.

"If I was defending Susie, I sure would try and point the finger of guilt at Johnny and the stun gun as much as possible. That will dilute the case against Susie and make the jury focus their attention on Johnny, rather than Susie. Since I'm a little iffy about Susie being convicted, as trustee, I'm holding back in reserve her 10% share of the trust and waiting to see if she's acquitted and entitled to receive the money.

"Under Oregon Law, a beneficiary is not entitled to receive any distribution from a decedent's trust if that beneficiary is responsible for the murder of the person who created the trust."

"Well, one good thing that came from Greg's unfortunate death is that we have a new friend, Jack. I'd met him a time or two over the years, but now I consider him to be a close friend of ours. I really like him and I know you do, too. That's a plus," Kelly said.

"Yes, and I do have some good news. Remember the waitress, Mitzi, at The Waterfront Restaurant?" Well, she called this afternoon and told me that her daughter received a full scholarship to the

University of Oregon, and she's thrilled. She's a good person, and although I've never met her daughter, I'm really happy for both of them."

"Mike, didn't you say something about getting a fee for being the trustee of Greg's trust? You sure have done a lot of work on it, and you deserve to be paid," Kelly said.

"I did, and I've already earmarked it for Kauai. Cash may think he's paying for our trip as a gift, but career military men don't make a lot of money. Considering what he could be earning if he was in the private workforce, it's a shame. I can't do much about that, but I darned sure can treat my stepson to a vacation, rather than the other way around."

"Woo-hoo! Bring on the mai tais!"

RECIPES

BAKED SALMON WITH TOMATO-ONION BÉRNAISE SAUCE

Ingredients:
4 salmon filets (about 6 oz. each)
1 tbsp. olive oil
4 tbsp. butter
½ cup finely chopped yellow onion
1 medium tomato, chopped
Milk, use amount required on sauce mix package
1 pkg. béarnaise sauce mix (I use Knorr.)
1 tbsp. small capers, rinsed and drained
Salt and freshly ground pepper to taste
Cooking spray

Directions:
Preheat oven to 425 degrees. Spray a small amount of cooking spray on the bottom of a shallow roasting pan. Arrange salmon in pan, skin side down. Brush with olive oil, season with salt and pepper, and bake 20 minutes. Remove from oven, peel skin off with fingers and scrape away "dark material" from under the skin using a thin spatula.

While salmon is baking, melt 2 tbsp. butter in a large frying pan and cook onions about 2-3 minutes over medium heat. Stir in milk.

Add chopped tomatoes, packet of béarnaise sauce mix, remaining 2 tbsp butter, and capers. Bring to a boil, reduce heat and stir constantly until sauce thickens, about 2-3 minutes. Pour sauce over salmon and serve. Enjoy!

MELONS & FRUIT IN SWEET YOGURT SAUCE

Ingredients:
6-8 oz. melon balls (cantaloupe, honeydew, or other)
6-8 oz. sliced fruit (bananas, berries, or other)
4 oz. blueberries
4 oz. raisins
8 oz. vanilla flavored Greek yogurt
3 heaping tsp. powdered sugar
3-4 tbsp. granola, slightly crushed
2 tbsp. cashew nuts, slightly crushed

Directions:
In a medium size mixing bowl combine the yogurt and powdered sugar. Stir until smooth. Add melon, fruit, raisins, and blueberries. Gently combine until fruit is covered with yogurt mixture. Combine the granola and cashew nuts in a separate bowl and set aside.

Spoon yogurt mixture into individual serving bowls and chill in refrigerator until ready to serve. Remove from refrigerator and sprinkle each bowl with equal amounts of the granola/cashew mixture. Serve immediately. Enjoy!

MIXED GREEN SALAD WITH SEARED AHI TUNA

Ingredients:
2 frozen Ahi tuna filets, 6 oz. each, thawed
14 oz. bag of mixed greens
6 Baby Bella mushrooms, stems on, thinly sliced
4 tbsp. blue cheese salad dressing (I use Bob's Big Boy. You may

want to use more.)
4 tbsp. blue cheese, crumbled
4 tbsp. sesame seeds
1 tbsp. olive oil

Directions:
Mix the greens, mushrooms, and blue cheese in a medium bowl. Toss to combine.

Sprinkle the sesame seeds on a dry plate and fully coat both sides of the Ahi filets with the seeds. (You may need to slightly moisten the filets with water so the sesame seeds will adhere to them.)

Add olive oil to medium size frying pan and heat on medium. Cook filets for 3-4 minutes, flipping over when bottom 1/3 of filet turns white. Cook other side 2-3 minutes. Remove from pan and cut filet into bite-size pieces. Place greens mixture on serving plates. Sprinkle fish on top of prepared salad and enjoy!

MINI CINNAMON ROLLS

Ingredients:
Rolls:
One 8 oz, tube crescent roll dough
2 tbsp. butter
Cinnamon to taste
Brown sugar to taste
Icing:
1 tsp. maple syrup
1 tbsp. milk
¾ cup powdered sugar
Nonstick cooking spray

Directions:
Preheat oven according to crescent roll package directions. Lay out half the dough (4 triangles) and pinch the seams together so they form a square. Flip over and pinch backsides seams.

Using a rolling pin, smooth the seams and roll the dough into a square about ¼" thick. Brush with half the butter and sprinkle on as much cinnamon and sugar as desired.

Roll into a log and cut into 8 pieces. Spray a mini muffin tin with the nonstick spray. Place the rolls into the tin. Repeat the process with the second half of the dough. Bake according to package directions.

Meanwhile whisk together the maple syrup and the milk in a bowl. Add in the powdered sugar until it reaches desired consistency. Drizzle over warm cinnamon rolls. Enjoy!

CARAMEL PECAN TURTLE BROWNIES

Ingredients:
1 cup unsalted butter, cut into bits
2 cups sugar
4 extra large eggs
1 cup unsweetened cocoa powder
1 cup all-purpose flour
One 14 oz. can condensed milk, La Lecheria by Nestle
2 cups pecan halves
Nonstick cooking spray

Directions:
Preheat oven to 350 degrees. Coat a 9" x 13" baking dish with nonstick spray. Combine the butter, sugar, and eggs in a food processor until smooth. Add the cocoa and pulse 4 or 5 times. Add the flour and pulse until it disappears into the mixture. Heat the condensed milk in the microwave in a bowl until it liquefies.

Spread half the chocolate batter over the bottom of the prepared pan. Spoon the La Lecheria over that and top with half the pecans. Top with the remaining chocolate batter. It's easier to dot the top of the La Lecheria layer with blobs of chocolate batter, rather than try to spread it evenly over the La Lecheria. Sprinkle the remaining pecans evenly over the top and bake until a skewer inserted into the center comes out with some crumbles and caramel on it, 30 – 35 minutes.

Remove from the oven, cut the brownies into squares, and leave them in the pan on a rack to cool completely. Enjoy!

LEAVE A REVIEW

I'd really appreciate it you could take a few seconds and leave a review of Death in the Bay.

Just go to the link below. Thank you so much, it means a lot to me ~ Dianne

http://getbook.at/DITB

Paperbacks & Ebooks for FREE

Go to www.dianneharman.com/freepaperback.html and get your FREE copies of Dianne's books and favorite recipes immediately by signing up for her newsletter.

Once you've signed up for her newsletter you're eligible to win three paperbacks. One lucky winner is picked every week. Hurry before the offer ends!

ABOUT THE AUTHOR

Dianne lives in Huntington Beach, California, with her husband, Tom, a former California State Senator, and her boxer dog, Kelly. Her passions are cooking, reading, and dogs, so whenever she has a little free time, you can either find her in the kitchen, playing with Kelly in the back yard, or curled up with the latest book she's reading. Her award-winning books include:

Cedar Bay Cozy Mystery Series

Cedar Bay Cozy Mystery Series - Boxed Set

Liz Lucas Cozy Mystery Series

Liz Lucas Cozy Mystery Series - Boxed Set

High Desert Cozy Mystery Series

High Desert Cozy Mystery Series - Boxed Set

Northwest Cozy Mystery Series

Northwest Cozy Mystery Series - Boxed Set

Midwest Cozy Mystery Series

Midwest Cozy Mystery Series - Boxed Set

Jack Trout Cozy Mystery Series

Cottonwood Springs Cozy Mystery Series

Cottonwood Springs Mystery Series – Boxed Set

Coyote Series

Midlife Journey Series - Midlife Journey Boxed Set

Red Zero Series - Black Dot Series

The Holly Lewis Mystery Series - Holly Lewis Boxed Set

Newsletter

If you would like to be notified of her latest releases please go to www.dianneharman.com and sign up for her newsletter.

Website: www.dianneharman.com,
Blog: www.dianneharman.com/blog
Email: dianne@dianneharman.com

PUBLISHING 11/27/19

TROUBLE AT THE NEW DAWN B & B

BOOK EIGHT OF

THE COTTONWOOD SPRINGS COZY MYSTERY SERIES

http://getbook.at/TAND

Days away from a grand opening

A long-awaited vision about to come true

Is thwarted by a computer hacker

When it works, modern technology is miraculous

When someone knows how to abuse it

It can mean the end of a dream

Brigid and Linc are clueless when it comes to computers. Good thing their daughter, Holly, knows a thing or two about them. Now if they can just find out who hacked the magnificent website she built and get it up and running again before it's too late and their beautiful B & B becomes nothing more than a vacant building with no visitors.

This is the eighth book in the Cottonwood Springs Cozy Mystery Series by a two-time USA Today Bestselling Author.

Open your smartphone, point and shoot at the QR code below. You will be taken to Amazon where you can pre-order 'Trouble at the New Dawn B & B'.

(Download the QR code app onto your smartphone from the iTunes or Google Play store in order to read the QR code below.)

Made in the USA
Monee, IL
07 July 2022